# A Widow's WISH

A Widow's Wish
Copyright © Caytlyn Brooke
All rights reserved.

No parts of this publication may be reproduced, distributed, or transmitted in any form or by any means, including photocopying, recording, or other electronic or mechanical methods without the prior written permission of the publisher, except in the case of brief quotations embodied in critical reviews and certain other noncommercial uses permitted by copyright law. For permission requests, please write to the publisher.

This book is a work of fiction. The characters, incidents, and dialogue are drawn from the author's imagination and are not to be construed as real. Any resemblance to actual events or persons, living or dead, is entirely coincidental.
First published by Kindle Direct Publishing 2025

First Edition
ISBN: 979-8-9877402-8-6 (Softcover)
ISBN: 979-8-9877402-9-3 (Ebook)

Visit Caytlyn Brooke's website:
http://caytlynbrooke.wixsite.com/booksbycaytlyn

Editor: Chelsea Cambeis
Cover Designer: Neil J Hart

## OTHER WORKS

Dark Flowers
Wired
Crimson Crisp
Among the Hunted
Among the Burning
Hush Little Baby
The Baker's Wife

A
Widow's
WISH

# CONTENT WARNING

This book contains explicit sexual content and is intended for mature readers ages 18 and up. There are mentions of suicide, blood, and death. If you or someone you know are struggling with suicidal thoughts or self-harm, please call or text 988 to speak with someone at the Suicide and Crisis Lifeline.

# CONTENTS

For Ainsley,
Thank you for being one of the first people to encourage me to keep writing romance. Make sure you have lots of batteries for this one . . .

13

"If you can't stand the heat, get out of the kitchen."
— Common Saying

# CHAPTER ONE

A dozen orderly soldiers gazed at the ceiling, sporting drizzled tattoos and piped smiles. Each was crafted from the finest gingerbread in three counties, fresh from the oven of the only explicit novelty bakery in rural Pennsylvania. The aroma of spiced dough and glazed treats captivated first-time customers, but it was the erotic details that had launched the little shop to national fame.

People from every corner of the state trekked to the brick bakery on the corner of Palmer Street to purchase one of the scandalous desserts. Aristocrats and blue-collar laborers alike desired the chance to peek behind the frosted curtains and select their gingerbread man. The cookies all stood at full attention, of course, their iced cocks sporting a variety of flavors: pistachio, red velvet, tiramisu, strawberry shortcake, mint julep, toasted caramel, triple fudge chocolate, apple pie, rum raisin, and of course, classic. Everyone wished to indulge in the sugared fantasy, to slip their lips around a phallic pastry without the restrictions of decorum and grace. Within the bakery's walls, people could detach from life's everyday stressors and explore the carnal curiosities 1909 society demanded they keep corseted and laced.

Unrestrained laughter and excited squeals billowed inside from open to close, but no matter how many customers delighted in her creations or how long the line snaked, Emma couldn't shake the crumb of failure lodged in the pit of her stomach each time she baked a new batch and the dough failed to rise. Not literally. Every cookie was baked to perfection. Still, no matter how large she molded the dough or how many recipes she tried, the magic that had wrought Cyn—her delicious and protective lover to life—refused to be conjured once more.

Emma exhaled her fleeting hope and batted her oven mitts to the floor. Two years. For two years she'd pounded and rolled and baked cookie after cookie with the prayer that Cyn would return. But every time the pan cooled, she was left alone, a large gingerbread man cookie with an impressive appendage grinning at her in pity.

That was her reason for taking over her late husband's shop. After Cyn's and Henry's violent ends, Emma had locked herself in the kitchen and churned out dozens of cookies in desperation. Soon, gingerbread littered every surface of her home. She'd only started storing the gingerbread at the shop to make room for more, terrified to discard in case the magic required a few days to stew.

Then, as luck or fate would have it, one of her neighbors had caught a glimpse of her creations while Emma was transporting them to the bakery and laughed until she turned red in the face. She bought it as a joke for her friend's fiftieth birthday, and then the craze for her naughty treats exploded. She sold every gingerbread man in the shop within twenty-four hours. Part of her yearned to turn all the business away and hoard her inanimate men far from prying eyes. What if another lonely woman bought one and Cyn came to life for *her*? Would he even remember Emma and their time together? Or would he just start life fresh with the first person he saw?

An icy breath froze her racing heart. She closed her eyes as a shiver climbed her spine. The memory of his warm hands caressed her curves and wove through her hair, pulling the strands back with just enough force to elicit a moan from her parted lips. What if the magic finally worked after years of hoping, only for someone else? Emma wouldn't be able to stand it.

Her bakery had been open for eighteen months now, though no startled screams of alarm had filled the space. Of course, when Cyn had first stepped into her kitchen in all his nude glory, his iced tattoos hypnotically serpentining around cords of muscle, drawing her eyes to the thick addition hanging between his legs—the one she herself had formed by squeezing and kneading the dough to perfection—she hadn't been able to utter much more than a choked whisper.

Her screams had come later. First, when he'd

chased her around the house and lain between her legs, plunging his skillful tongue inside her aching center. Again, when he'd bent her over the counter after they spilled that bag of flour. A fine mist had drifted through the air like a snow flurry, coating them both in a grainy shimmer, and he'd pounded his length into her relentlessly, his wide palms spreading her ass so he could stare at his cock as it glided in and out of her. Then once more, when he'd pinned her against the doorframe. One hand had cradled her leg, baring her cunny to him, while his other encircled her throat, clutching hard enough to bruise. She'd gasped for breath as Cyn coaxed her further and further over the edge toward one of the most powerful orgasms she'd ever experienced. She'd screamed for Henry to hear. Cyn had demanded it—demanded she cry *his* name so her husband would know he no longer owned her. She belonged to herself and decided who she shared her body with.

Emma fought to keep the next flood of memories at bay, but the dam she'd thrust them behind cracked and leaked. Flashes of Henry storming in to find them entwined, Cyn's cock buried deep in her pussy, burst behind her eyes. Her husband's cardamom-colored face alive with fury, the shotgun in his hands. Cyn had charged him, and the carnage that ensued was straight out of a horror novel—blood and bone and crumbling gingerbread splintered to irregular chunks showering in a grisly multicolored spray. She'd been the only one still breathing after the violent affair, left to clean up the gruesome scene, along with her mangled heart.

Emma tossed her head to rid herself of the ghosts. It didn't pay to dwell on the past. It only brought further heartbreak. Her failure with every bake already rendered enough misery. She plunged her hands back into the sticky dough. Flour encircled her wrists and blanketed her freckled forearms. The heady sweet scent of molasses wafted with each knead, followed by the comforting blend of ginger and cinnamon. By all appearances, the cozy back room was effervescent with happiness, yet Emma couldn't shake the constant throb of grief that nettled and stuck beneath her ribs like a stubborn bur. She didn't want to admit it, but she was losing hope she'd ever be able to craft the same magic that blessed her that day and brought Cyn to her.

The encounter with the gingerbread man had ruined her. The idea of dating any of the men in town soured her stomach. How could they possibly compare to Cyn? To the incredible world of lust and passion he'd opened her eyes to? Her marriage to Henry had been arranged. Transactional. Henry was an old man intrigued by her beauty and youth, and her father couldn't wait to be rid of her, so he'd sold her to the highest bidder.

Henry was cruel and condescending, inflicting pain to manipulate and control, whereas Cyn taught her how good she could feel. How to tease and taste until she was unable to contain her pleasure a moment longer. She wanted that back. God, how she wanted him back.

The first man who'd ever looked at her and actually saw her, and he wasn't even real. Just her luck.

She rolled the thickening dough over and over until a firm sphere formed under her hands. Emma moved it to an open counter beside her mother's rolling pin. The utensil held conflicting emotions for her. Henry had abused her knuckles with its unyielding bite, but she'd also relished the hard wood's kiss when it was under Cyn's command, striking her ass with such fervor she'd yelped. Surprisingly, *that* pain was electrifying, waking her up after so long of being hurt by her husband. She now yearned for the release Cyn's spanks and pinches and thrusts had brought about, along with the gentle massages and licks he'd administered afterward. He made her feel alive, like a whole new person capable of indulging in all the erotic fantasies she hadn't even known existed. Like Bluebeard's forbidden door, once she'd unlocked and explored the secrets inside, there was no going back.

The bell above the door chimed. Emma stilled and set the rolling pin aside. Rounding the corner, she exited into the front of the bakery to the narrow walkway behind the display case. A well-dressed man in a brown bowler hat lingered by the door, a slender mahogany cane hooked over his forearm. Only his profile was visible, but she took an instant dislike to his hawk-like nose and severe jawline that could have been carved from glass. Unease rippled through her, setting her teeth on edge. His aura was reminiscent of Henry's. A predator on the hunt.

Emma dusted her hands on the front of her apron and leaned against the case. "Good morning, sir. What can I get for you today? The maple frosted cookies are fresh from the oven."

A scoff echoed as the gentleman sauntered closer, his gait light and confident. "Not today, I'm afraid. I'm here regarding a more delicate matter."

The hairs on the back of her neck prickled. "Delicate?"

The man grinned, looking wolfish and hungry. "Yes. The matter concerns your . . . charming little shop. You see, my uncle was Henry Abbot. Your late husband, I believe."

Emma pressed her lips into a firm line. "Yes. I'm Henry's widow. What is your name?"

"Nicoli Dunst." He didn't extend his hand in greeting but maintained eye contact as if daring her to look away.

Emma kept her face expressionless. "I'm sorry for your loss."

"Same for you. You must have been . . . devastated when Uncle passed so suddenly." His dark chestnut irises slid from side to side. "I wasn't aware he was so depressed that he would decide to take his own life—and in such a violent manner."

Emma tilted her head. "Neither was I, but Henry kept his emotions very close to his chest. I wish I had been able to see the sadness he was struggling with."

"Indeed," Nicoli said with a quick arch of his eyebrow.

Silence stretched, heavy and uncomfortable with everything they weren't saying. "Henry never mentioned you. In fact, I never met any of his family during the time we were married."

"I've been traveling in Europe the last few years after attending university."

"Uh-huh. And now you're back?"

Nicoli smirked. "And now I'm back."

Emma tried to keep her eyes from rolling at the nephew's smugness. He refused to volunteer the point of his visit. No. He was the sort of man who withheld on purpose if only to let the other party flounder before his eyes, but she had experience with men like him. Henry had abused her from the time she was forced to move into his home.

Straightening, Emma beamed a toothy grin at the dapper man and skipped over the question Mr. Dunst so obviously wished to draw from her. "Well, thanks for introducing yourself, but I have half a dozen orders to fill, so if you'll excuse me . . ." She turned her back to him, then flinched when a sharp rap on the glass case resounded in reply. When Emma whipped back around, the bastard's cane was poised slightly above the display case, and his gaze threatened that he would hit it again—this time with more force.

"Our conversation has not concluded," Nicoli seethed through poorly veiled gritted teeth. "You see, after my dear uncle passed, the estate and this bakery were bequeathed to you, but only because Henry's closest living *male* relative couldn't be located."

Emma's stomach tightened and her mouth went dry. "Correct. The lawyers signed the estate and Henry's meager assets over to me as his spouse."

"Yes, but in the case that a male relative returned and desired the estate, it would revert back to said individual, as women are not capable of owning property or running a business."

"Now, hold on! I'm doing very well on my own. Profits have skyrocketed since I took over the bakery, and my overhead has remained consistent. I was even featured in *Ladies Magazine's* profile on their Top 10 Influential Businesswomen just last week."

Nicoli's eyes glazed with contempt. "So I read. The article is what prompted my visit to this backwoods little town, actually."

"Which translates to you saw my success and wanted to cash in on it. What happened? Spend all your money gambling and now you need an easy way to fill your pockets?"

Nicoli crossed his arms and pursed his lips. "You know, you're not nearly as vapid as your photo led me to believe. But like it or not, the situation is as such. I now own this bakery and every future cent it earns."

A snarl erupted behind Emma's teeth. "You can't be serious. Now that Henry's gone, this is the only income I have. Do you even know how to bake?"

Nicoli replaced his cane over his forearm and removed the bowler from his head, revealing thick greasy blond waves slicked back over his scalp. "How's this, then, my fair aunt? I will allow you to continue working at *my* bakery and even pay you a modest sum so you can buy yourself some pretty little baubles. You can even keep your home . . ."

Emma's heart lurched as she waited for the other shoe to drop. Again, Nicoli took his time, savoring her unease as the tension built between them.

"You know, since, as owner of the estate, your home shall also become mine, and though I doubt I could ever replace my uncle, your loving husband, know that I will spend every night beside you, loving you as a woman should be loved by a man."

Emma's spine trembled with fear. "I don't want any part of this or you."

Nicoli placed the bowler snugly back into place and jutted his whiskery chin in her direction. "You don't have a choice, dear. I'm off to get my request signed by a judge. Tomorrow, our new life begins." He spun atop his well-worn shoes and exited the shop, slamming the door behind him.

Emma glanced around at whatever she had within arm's reach and grabbed the heaviest object she could find. Rage thrummed through her veins, and she heaved the bulky wooden cylinder at the spot Nicoli's head had occupied seconds before. The instrument crashed against the front window with a resounding thwack and dropped to the floorboards in a distinctive double-patter.

Anger dissolved into dread as the red film rescinded from Emma's sight and she realized with horrifying clarity that the missile she'd walloped at the door was none other than her mother's rolling pin.

She rounded the cash register and hurried toward the two separate pieces on the floor. Her heart broke with a jagged slice that matched the broken end of the rolling pin where the right handle used to be attached. There was nothing to be done. No way to mend her grievous mistake.

Emma gathered both pieces to her chest, and fat unrestrained tears slid down the smooth body of the cylinder. The last of her mother's treasures, and she'd destroyed it. Regret, guilt, and fury at her own temper stormed inside her, and she unleashed a ragged scream. It wasn't fair. It wasn't *fair*! Finally, she'd escaped her terrible husband only for him to be replaced by an equally horrid nephew. She held no fantasies about what her new forced marriage would entail. Even in their brief meeting, she'd discerned the kind of narcissistic man Nicoli was: a man used to getting his way and cutting down anyone who dared oppose him.

The clock chimed, announcing midday. As much as Emma wanted to remain curled on the floor wallowing in self-pity, she was still the owner of her bakery—for one more day, at least—and she had orders to fill.

# CHAPTER TWO

Emma set down the shattered rolling pin next to the pile of dough she'd been kneading for Ms. Jenkin's bachelorette party. Without bothering to wipe away her tears, she sprinkled a pinch of flour on top of the dough. She held the drum of the pin and began to carefully roll it back and forth, pressing the mound down into a flat sheet.

Several times, the pin curved or jerked at an awkward angle as she struggled to guide it over the bumps, but if she maintained pressure on the outskirts of the drum, she could still use it. A jolt of joy and relief surged in Emma's chest. She hadn't ruined it after all! Crouching to inspect the dough at counter level, she noticed it was too thick. She put the rolling pin down atop an errant pile of crushed ginger and ripped the ball in half, then smooshed it into two separate rounded spheres. Perfect. She could utilize the extra for Mrs. Fowler's order.

Once the dough had been re-kneaded, rolled, and smoothed to a proper thickness, Emma traced the shape of her signature gingerbread man, including head, arms, legs, and of course his behemoth cock. With the first gingerbread man ready for the oven, she quickly manipulated the residual dough and formed a slightly smaller gingerbread man on a second tray.

Emma slid the double trays into the oven and set the timer. Two orders done. She focused her attention next on the three dozen mini-gingerbread men for a party at the retirement home. She wished she could be there to see the residents' reactions to the little penises. Hopefully, no one would go into cardiac arrest.

While her hands kneaded, mixed, rolled, and decorated, curious new customers stumbled in alongside seasoned fans. Emma's thoughts whirled and revolved, looking for a solution to the very real problem that had quite literally knocked on her door. The sunlight that drenched the front windows glowed with an apricot haze. The short hand of the large clock out front neared the four. One more hour and then she'd be able to close and head to the library. Maybe she'd discover some hidden clause or loophole amidst all the legal jargon of the estate paperwork.

Guiding the piping bag in delicate curlicues, Emma completed the iced design along the second gingerbread man's arms. Her men had long cooled. The first was maple cinnamon flavored and the second chocolate espresso. Sweet snowflakes. No two were alike, but unlike traditional cookies, she left off the cutesy spiced gumdrops. Though she appreciated the vibrancy the colors brought, she wasn't in the market of baking cute gingerbread. Cyn had been covered in edible ink, the icing adhering to his aromatic skin during the magical transition from cookie to man, and she couldn't bring herself to deviate from those details.

Emma's cookies looked cool, powerful, and almost dangerous. Her goal with every bake was to evoke that forbidden lust Cyn had awakened in her. Her patrons wanted to feel out of their element, naughty even. Cute smiles and pastel candies were for more family-friendly bakers.

Setting the near-empty piping bag on the counter, Emma threaded her fingers and lifted her hands over her head. She arched her back in a feline stretch and moaned as her tight muscles elongated after hours hunched in decorating mode. Rolling her neck, she sighed, proud of all the orders she'd accomplished on top of her regular inventory. She ran the tip of her finger along the outline of the first gingerbread man's elegantly iced shaft, and her tongue flicked out. The heady flavors burst on her taste buds. The icing hadn't quite set, and her nail smudged the line just the smallest bit.

Emma groaned around her finger and then extracted it from between her lips with an audible pop. "Don't worry. I can fix that."

The brass bell pealed, followed by impish laughter. Snapping to attention, Emma quickly stuck her hands under the faucet and added a dash of soap, then hurried out into the front lobby. Three women, barely old enough to satisfy the eighteen-year-old age requirement she'd pasted on the door, flocked to the display case, giggles erupting behind gloved hands and lace fans. Emma steeled herself.

"Oh! Celia, look at this one!"

"It's positively gigantic!"

"Mallory, think you could take all of this one?"

The trio pointed and cackled as they perused the contents of the case. It was several minutes before they even registered Emma was standing there.

"Oh! Dear Jesus, I didn't see you there!" one of the blondes exclaimed when her gaze finally connected with Emma's.

"That's because you're in heaven before all these frosted cocks, Abigail," the one with a splattering of freckles teased.

"For shame, Celia!" Abigail swatted her friend's arm and then demurred back to Emma with a slight blush. "I'm just curious, is all. My mama would *die* if she knew I'd stepped foot in here, but she's out of town visiting my grandmother, so my friends dragged me along. Do you bake these all yourself?"

Emma smiled and relaxed, remembering what it felt like to be so naïve. "I do indeed. It started as a joke for my late husband, but—"

A sudden calamity exploded in the back room as multiple tin pans popped. One even sounded as if it'd tipped onto the floor. Emma's heart sank. If one of the large gingerbread men orders had fallen, she'd be all right, but not two. She didn't have time to remake them both.

Three sets of eyes stared guiltily at her as if the girls' laughter had been the cause. Emma held up her hands and backed away. "Excuse me for just one moment." The young women nodded and dissolved into another fit when Celia mouthed something under her breath.

Rounding the corner, Emma was taken aback by the mess that greeted her. Crumbs, sugar, and flour covered the tables, prep space, and floor, while a curtain of the grainy mixture hung in the air, giving everything the hazy appearance of looking through a veil. Bowls of ground ginger and dark brown sugar were upended, their contents scattered across sticks of softened butter and pots of salt and ground cloves.

The tray that held the dozens of smaller gingerbread men was undisturbed, but the other two that hosted the larger men were both knocked to the floor. Emma raced over and slid to her knees. She grimaced as the cooled crumbs bit through her thin stockings. Carefully, she flipped the tray closest to her over and braced for the damage. Nothing but a shower of crumbs greeted her.

Her heart sank, but this didn't make sense. How could the cookie have crumbled so completely and into such minuscule uniform pieces? Emma dragged her hand to cup the crumbs and molded them into a tiny pile. It wasn't enough. If the whole cookie had shattered, there should have been more debris.

Emma reached and righted the second tray. A similar scene met her searching gaze. Both cookies were gone, not simply broken. She dropped to her palms and angled her face parallel to the floor. If the trays had popped from trapped heat, the force may have been strong enough to catapult the gingerbread men a sizable distance. It was too dark to check beneath the stove or the icebox. Besides, if they'd made it under there, they wouldn't be salvageable anyway.

Crestfallen, Emma pushed off the floor and climbed to her feet. Could this day get any worse? Another obnoxious clang of laughter billowed forth from the juvenile trio up front. Emma had to get back out there, had to adopt a cheerful façade when really, her heart was breaking. So much work. So much time she'd expended, and for nothing. Now, she was even further behind, with a mountain of work to redo before that despicable man returned tomorrow morning. She brushed the clinging crumbs and wasted spices from her hands onto the front of her apron and returned to the front with a subdued groan.

"Everything all right back there?" the one with the pinned red hat, Mallory, asked.

Emma stuck her hands in the sink basin and turned on the water after she lathered up. "Oh, sure. I just left my pans too close to the edge of the counter, and they fell."

"Oh dear." Celia clutched a hand to her chest. "Is everything ruined?"

Emma turned off the water and dried her hands. "Not everything, but enough that I'll be here for the rest of the night."

Abigail wrinkled her nose at the mention of extended labor. She didn't strike Emma as the kind of girl who'd ever worked a hard day in her life. "All night? Why don't you have a helper? Don't most shops have employees?"

"They do." Emma nodded. "And hiring an assistant is on my list. It's just getting to that point on the list that's the tricky part." She laughed softly and gestured to the baked goods in the display. "So have you ladies decided what you'd like to try?"

Celia pointed with a manicured nail to the right of the case toward a small gingerbread man with molasses frosting and almond décor. "That one, please. He looks . . . delicious."

"His cock is also nearly to his knees," Abigail chided. "I thought he had three legs when I looked the first time. Now who's being the dirty one?"

"What? Molasses frosting is my favorite. I can't help it if I have a sweet tooth."

"Sure, you little strumpet."

The girls chuckled once more. This time, they didn't bother to shield their wide brays and gleaming teeth. Emma nodded and bent at the waist to extract the desired cookie. "Did you only want one?"

The trio's wild laughter halted abruptly. Emma peered through the glass for an answer to her question, but the young women were no longer looking in her direction. Instead, all three of them stared ahead, their mouths agape as expressions of surprise, wonder, and uncertainty warred on their features. Emma tried to turn but only saw shadows as the dim bulb threw colorful orbs across her vision.

She began to withdraw from the display case when a solid heat pressed against her skirt. Emma flinched at the unexpected touch and slammed the side of her head against the ceiling of the case. "Ow! Ladies, you can't come back here—" she scolded, but all three of them remained firmly planted in their original positions, jaws still slack. Emma turned over her shoulder, suddenly alarmed. Had Nicoli come back early?

A hand larger than any hand had a right to be slipped beneath her skirt and cupped her ass, the palm tracing the swell of her curves. The man's audacity infuriated her. How dare he treat her like this? Like he owned her. And in front of customers!

"Listen, you little—" Emma's words shriveled to a strangled gasp when her head completed its rotation. The man behind her was not Henry's sniveling nephew. The man behind her was a giant the color of rich mahogany wood. Cords of muscle stood out starkly beneath a tight white shirt, and the thin cloth strained around his biceps. An apron had been hastily wrapped around his hips, riding low to expose the deep 'V' leading down to his pelvis. Was he nude underneath? Tattoos rippled in twisting swirls across his skin and drew her eye this way and that, a never-ending maze that captivated her attention. An eerie feeling teased the back of her mind like déjà vu. The strokes were familiar in both rhythm and execution.

The stranger's hand slid to the front of Emma's thigh, and the pad of his thumb stroked the soft flesh in soothing circles. "Hey, sugarcane."

# CHAPTER THREE

The aroma of cinnamon hit her with almost more force than those four simple syllables.

"Cyn? How?" Emma whispered. Tears welled in the basins of her eyelids and her chest tightened with relief, astonishment, joy, and shock. Every instinct compelled her to throw herself into Cyn's arms and mould her body against his warm chest, but a trio of customers remained, watching with vivid interest.

The women composed themselves at last and their gawking stares were replaced by clucking tongues and heavy judgment whirled at Emma's back.

"I thought you didn't have any staff?" Celia said. Her lips curled devilishly.

For a moment, Emma froze. Could these gossips see the resemblance between Cyn and the rest of the gingerbread men displayed before them? Was the magic detectable? Like sugar crystals in the air?

Emma spun around, doing her best to block Cyn from view, but her attempt was pointless. He was too big, too tall, too hot to shield from their hungry gazes.

Before she could answer, Cyn's other hand joined beneath her skirt. His fingers rubbed the length of her slit over her tights. The heat radiating from his touch alone was enough to make her wet. An arduous gasp crossed her lips as lust stirred at the apex of her thighs. Her body remembered his touch, yearned for the pleasure it knew he could bestow.

"Technically, I'm not staff. I'm a close friend of Emma's. I knew she was shorthanded today and volunteered my services. I'm Cyn."

"Yes, you are." Abigail swallowed. "Do you, um . . . live around here?"

Cyn shook his head. "No, ma'am. My brother and I are only visiting." He spoke so calmly, yet all the while, his touch intensified and centered on her clit, rubbing in glorious repetition. It was everything Emma could do to suppress the moan climbing her throat, but something made her pause.

"Brother?" Emma asked in synchrony with Mallory.

"There are two of you?" the young woman continued. She looked Cyn up and down like she wanted to take a bite. Thankfully, she couldn't see the way his hand grabbed Emma's ass, pinching the thick skin and then caressing the slight sting away. The case blocked their forbidden antics, but if he kept it up much longer, her orgasm wouldn't be as easy to hide.

"Yes. Although my junior, he'd argue he's the better looking of the two of us."

Mallory scoffed. "Oh, I can't see how that's possible."

"Where are you from?" Celia asked.

"All over. Now, did you ladies need anything else today?" His words were kind, but from the intensity with which his fingers moved, Emma could tell his patience for the young customers was growing thin. He pressed harder. For a moment, she thought he'd rip right through her tights to dip a finger into her warmth. They were her best pair, but right then, she wasn't above destroying them. Her sex clenched as her hips rocked, desperate for more.

Emma cleared her throat. "Y-Yes. Do you need anything else or just the one cookie?"

Cyn cupped her pussy, rubbing his hand faster to create the delicious friction she craved. Surely, her eyes were bulging out of her head. It felt so good. With a wicked thought, Emma realized she loved the thrill of being felt up publicly. It was the kinkiest act she'd ever engaged in and that was saying something, given her encounter with Cyn last time.

"Just the molasses-frosted man, please." Celia's cheeks blushed a deep carmine. Could she see the naughty things Cyn was doing or was she just shy purchasing the phallic pastry?

"Of course. Let me ring you up." Emma placed the gingerbread man in a discreet brown paper bag and folded the top over with a sharp crease. With a regrettable tap on Cyn's forearm, she stepped away from his touch and toward the register.

Out of the corner of her eye, she watched him to ensure he didn't crumble into sugary bits again. This time would be different. This time he wouldn't leave her. Fear spiked in her heart all the same, though. Without his hands on her, it was difficult to believe he was even there.

Emma punched in the correct numbers and read the total aloud. "Forty-two cents, please."

Celia opened her coin purse and withdrew the proper money. The register pinged and the drawer opened like a wagging tongue.

"Thank you," Emma said with a smile. "I hope you enjoy it. Come again, ladies."

"Now that you have . . . help, we'll be sure to return," Mallory called. "Have a productive day." She arched her manicured brows while a smirk danced on her lips. Maybe Emma's reactions to Cyn's touch hadn't been as cleverly masked as she'd hoped.

"Yes, for sure," Emma replied. She had no idea if her response was an adequate answer to the young woman's statement, but it didn't matter. She had bigger things to worry about.

The second the bell stilled after their departure, Emma rounded on Cyn and rushed back into his arms. "How did you get here?" She buried her face in his pectorals. "Why now? What finally brought you back?"

Cyn's warm palm stroked the back of her head. Gently, he pulled her away from his body so he could look into her teary amber eyes. "Shh, sugarcane. I'll answer all your questions, but first, I want to put a smile on your face and hear more of those gasps and moans—without you holding back."

Emma's lips parted. One minute she was staring into Cyn's dark eyes, and the next he'd scooped her up and set her on the counter beside the register. Eager hands pushed her sable skirt over her hips, and in the same swift motion, he yanked her tights off and pulled the thin panties that covered her pussy aside to bare her glistening slit. She barely had time to inhale before Cyn's tongue dove between her folds, parting her with restrained ferocity. He licked and kissed, each touch growing harder until she jerked beneath his passionate onslaught and threw her head back so far her braid grazed the countertop. Her knees parted, urging his skillful mouth to caress even more.

A guttural groan built in the back of her throat as her breasts heaved, aching for attention. Moans filled the air. Emma reached down and cradled Cyn's bald head closer to her pussy as her tornado of lust began to crest.

"Yes, Cyn. Fuck, I missed you." As if she'd spoken the magic words, Cyn shifted his tongue to her clit and sucked while he plunged three fingers inside her. "Fuck!"

Emma hissed in appreciation and her eyes squeezed tight in wondrous ecstasy. Between the heat from his mouth, combined with the steady thrum of his fingers, she was delirious with sensation. Faster, Cyn worked her clit, relentless in his delivery. She was powerless as her climax built, blinding her to all other thoughts. She was fully aware she was half-naked on her front counter, splayed out in full view of the large glass windows with her fictional gingerbread man between her thighs, but she didn't care. Finally, the ache in her chest was healing, and though she held little hope that whatever magic had returned her sweet Cyn to her would last, she was going to let go and enjoy every single moment they were given.

The glorious surge within seized and imploded, racing toward release. A wild groan fell from Emma's lips, and her spine arched as she shuddered with pleasure. Cyn's hold on her hip tightened as he drank her in, not pausing his tongue's tempo even when numerous almost violent waves rippled through her frame. Already, she could feel another orgasm rushing toward her beneath Cyn's punishing pace.

A long shadow darkened the space behind her eyelids, accompanied by a spear of warmth against her cheek. Acting on instinct, Emma's lips parted, and Cyn's cock slid over her tongue, not stopping until it hit the back of her throat. She choked on the length but remembered Cyn's instructions all those months ago. Inhaling through her nose, she relaxed. Her lips wrapped around the thick shaft while she swallowed him deeper.

"Oh fuck. I thought you said she was inexperienced?"

A deep baritone thundered above her, an unfamiliar cadence compared to Cyn's warm timbre. Emma's eyes flew open, but all she could see was a dark chestnut wall as their hips thrust into her mouth. That's when she realized. The angle was off. If Cyn was crouched at her feet, playing between her thighs, he'd never be able to fill her mouth with his cock. Which meant . . . she had someone else down her throat.

# CHAPTER FOUR

Emma bucked her hips and twisted her head away, effectively ending whatever orgy she'd unwillingly participated in. Wrenching down her skirt, she pushed herself into a sitting position and threw up her hands. "What the hell is going on?"

Cyn stared at her with an apologetic expression, but his eyes resembled burning coals when his gaze lifted to the silhouette behind her. "I told you to stay in the back." He straightened, his chin shiny with the evidence of the pleasure he'd given her.

"I was bored. Besides, it sounded like you were having some fun out here, and I wanted a taste. You were right. She's a rare dollop of sweet cream, but you failed to mention how . . . eager she is."

"Enough, Cris," Cyn barked.

Emma turned, ready to lay into the entitled newcomer, but her words stuck fast in her throat. Another gingerbread man stood framed by the giant window, a wall of muscle and tattoos. He was stockier than Cyn, but he looked as if he could take on a freight train and win. He was also stark naked, save for a satisfied smirk on his lips and the shine of Emma's saliva encircling the crown of his dark shaft. Fully erect, every inch of his cock was branded with dark chocolate swirls.

Unconsciously, Emma ran her tongue along her lower lip. Chocolate espresso was heady on her taste buds. Why didn't she realize sooner? They each had their own unique flavor . . . just the way she'd designed them. A memory of Cyn's earlier comment sparked in her mind.

"Is this your brother?" Emma rounded on Cyn.

"Yeah. This is Cris. He was *supposed* to stay in the kitchen. I never meant for him to take advantage of you like that."

"But how did he get here? How did you both come alive this time? What did I do differently?"

Cyn hooked his palms around the outside of Emma's thighs and pulled her forward so that her ass was nearly off the counter. He stepped between her knees and held her close. "It was your tears."

Emma gave an unladylike snort. "I don't think so. Believe me, that was not the first time I've cried into batter trying to bring you back."

Cyn traced her jaw with his nose and planted gentle kisses along her skin. Desire stirred once more at his sensual touch. "But it was never about wanting me. The first time the magic worked, you didn't even know my existence was possible. Your tears stemmed from something else." He tucked a stray tendril of hair behind her ear, then, using the pad of his thumb, brushed her cheekbone with tenderness, as if *she* might shatter.

Emma's thoughts whirled back to that fateful morning when her entire world had changed. She'd worked through the night, baking and forming the giant gingerbread cookie for her husband. There had been pain and hurtful words, but that was a normal occurrence with Henry. The past flashed, rewinding further, hoping to present the events to her again in a way that she might understand this time.

She pushed her memory harder than she'd ever tried, analyzing the events *before* Henry burdened her with the cruel task rather than her actions afterward. There was a sharp slap to her cheek when she pointed out that the dough needed to chill. Orders fell like rain after Henry demanded she roll and cut out the cookies. He'd ripped her mother's tin cutter from her grasp and thrown it at the wall on his way to bed—a final terror to haunt her as he made his departure.

Emma's heart ached as she pictured the broken cutter, the thin metal unable to withstand the impact. She'd allowed her tears to fall then as well, grieving for herself and her mother. Realization dawned.

"My rolling pin."

"What?" Cyn asked.

"Right before I made you, I was arguing with a horrible relation of my late husband's, and without thinking, I hurled my mother's rolling pin at the door. The handle broke off, and I wept over my stupidity.

You're right. It was never about you. It was losing a piece of my mother. That's the connection. You came to comfort me."

"Always, sugar. I only wish I could have found my way to you sooner."

Emma's gaze wandered to the second man. "But why did you come to life, too?" She exhaled. All the flickering thoughts made her dizzy. The past rushed like a sped-up silent film behind her eyes. The rolling pin wasn't strong enough to roll out the thick dough, so she'd torn a chunk off and molded a second smaller cookie for Mrs. Fowler's order rather than mixing a separate batch. Both portions of dough had been smoothed by the pin saturated in tears.

The memory of the popping pans echoed. Both men had come to life because both had been created with the rolling pin and the sorrow over its destruction.

Emma eyed Cris. His erection had softened as the heat of the moment cooled, but his cock was still an impressive length as it settled. She turned back to Cyn. "I can't believe you're back." Her heart beat with joy, and her eyes misted again.

"Now, now," Cyn admonished gently. "No more sad tears. How can we help? I heard you mention you had lots of orders to fill?"

A dry laugh escaped Emma's throat. "Yes, especially now that my orders have chosen to come to life. I need to get them re-baked before morning. Otherwise . . ." Her words trailed off as her gaze grew steely.

Cyn frowned. "What's wrong?"

A dejected sigh rushed from her lips. "My husband's nephew. He just showed up and claimed the bakery and my house are his now. Rightfully inherited after Henry's death because women are prohibited from owning property if a male heir is alive and competent."

"What?" Cyn spat. "After everything that terrible man did to you? That can't be right."

Emma shrugged. "Nicoli has gone to see the judge regarding the papers. Starting tomorrow, he owns all I make and—" She fumbled for how to phrase the rest. Cyn's protectiveness was so strong the last time he'd come to her. So intense that he'd fought Henry for the right to be with her and took a shotgun blast trying to defend her from her husband's fury. She shuddered to think what sort of violence her admission might set off this time once her lover learned Henry's nephew intended not only to take up his role as her boss, but husband as well.

"And what, sugarcane?" Cyn asked. "What aren't you telling me?"

Emma squeezed his arms that held her as if she could anchor his temper. "He means to move into my house—and take me as his wife in Henry's stead."

"No!" Cyn smashed his fist into one of the nearby cupboards. The hinge squeaked open in surrender. "He can't have you!"

"What do you propose I do? Common law grants men control over women. They'd laugh me out of court if I tried to defend myself, or worse throw me in an institution for refusing to comply."

Cris stepped toward the counter and punched a fist into the palm of his opposite hand. "Then we wait for him to come back and kill him like Cyn killed your husband."

"Another body isn't the answer," Cyn growled, but it was obvious he'd had a similar thought.

"We can't do nothing," Cris argued.

"True, but we also can't be rash. We need to make a solid plan first." Cyn glanced at the clock. "What time did he say he'd return tomorrow?"

"I'm not sure. The bakery opens at eight. I can't imagine he'd delay very long."

"All right. To start, we need to get your other orders made. That'll give us time to think, too," Cyn rationalized.

"Yes," Emma whispered, glad to have a small sliver of direction. She reached onto her toes and wrapped her arms around Cyn's neck, pulling him down to her lips. Another wave of desire roiled within her when his heavenly scent ensnared her thoughts. She knew she should be concerned about completing her workload, should be focused on the mounting issues ahead, but every part of her was far too excited to properly care.

After two years and countless attempts, Cyn was back, standing firm and real beside her. Now that her heart was healed like a cracked cookie mended with a slathering of sweet frosting, other areas of her body yearned for attention. Emma's lips parted Cyn's with fervor. Her small moan breathed along his tongue as she pulled his lower lip between her teeth. Instantly,

Cyn responded. His large hands slid down to cradle her ass, squeezing just hard enough to sting.

"Yes." Emma sighed. She pressed the length of her body against Cyn's torso, subtly rubbing his chest with her breasts while her leg hiked north to wrap around his hip.

His erection sprang to attention, spearing her in the stomach with a blaze of warmth. Suddenly, Emma realized how scantily clad Cyn was, with nothing but a thin shirt and a hastily secured apron covering his eager shaft. With a quick slide of the strings and a tug of her skirt, his glorious crown would find her. The mere memory of how his cock had filled her made her center quiver and ache with need. His tattoos had felt like textured ridges when he'd thrust into her, then teased her with the weeping tip before driving himself back in. Lord, she needed him now.

Their kisses turned hard, full of biting teeth and exploring tongues as they became reacquainted with each other's bodies. Emma ran her hands along Cyn's broad shoulders while he bent his head and nibbled her earlobe, dropping fiery kisses along the curve of her neck. As if sharing thoughts, Cyn pushed Emma's skirt up over her waist and ripped her panties down to where they puddled on the tops of her feet. She shifted a step to rid herself of them, and Cyn grazed the soft curls covering her. He slipped one finger inside, testing, teasing, preparing her for his cock. She was already wet, desperate for him.

His lips found hers once more when he added another finger. Emma growled in the back of her throat, unable to help herself. Reaching down, she undid the apron's tie to expose Cyn's throbbing cock. Had she made it even bigger this time?

Wrapping her hand around the shaft, she giggled. The heat of him felt just like a cookie fresh from the oven, but there was no softness or threat of being underbaked. Cyn was hard and thick, perfect.

"Fuck, sugarcane. I can barely take it when you touch me like that," Cyn muttered against her lips. Using his other hand, he cradled the back of her head and tangled his long fingers in the messy waves above her low braid.

"Really? What about when I do this?" Guiding the head of his cock to her slit, Emma arched back and rubbed his crown along her pussy, thrusting her hips to meet his.

"Fuck." Cyn pulled her hair, his touch growing rough. He pulled his fingers out and rubbed her wetness along his length before palming the tip. "Are you ready for me, sugar? Ready for me to bury this big cock in your sweet little cunt?"

"Yes, Cyn. I've waited so long for you. Please fuck me."

"I love it when you beg, when you moan my name. Is this what you want?"

Emma slid her cunt faster along his crown, pushing it into her center just the slightest bit. "Yes, yes. I need you to fuck me."

Cyn took hold of his shaft, pumping the skin up and down in a slow rhythm. "So eager," he said with a grin. "That's my girl."

Without warning, he flipped her over and smacked her ass, then planted a sweet kiss to dull the pain. Unlike last time when the pain had caught her off guard, now it woke her up, further proof that her lover was real again. The rough spank electrified her lust. All those months of being alone, of mourning the connection she'd made with Cyn, of knowing what she was missing, made her passion that much more explosive now that she had the chance to act on it.

Emma placed her hands on either side of her ass and spread her flesh. "Show me how much you missed me, big boy."

"Fuck." Cyn drawled out the word, mesmerized. The heat of his cock skimmed her inner thighs just before the crown split her slit.

"Did you seriously forget I'm standing right here?" Cris asked, breaking the intensity of the moment. "I mean, don't get me wrong, I love watching, but I'd much rather play, especially with such a luscious little vanilla chip."

Emma gasped, clutching a hand over her heart. "Oh shit. I just, um . . . Well, I lost track of everything else."

Cyn groaned behind her. He eased the tip of his cock away from her cunny and hastily pulled down her skirt. "Great timing, Cris. Couldn't you have just hung out in the back?"

"And miss the show? No way. Though it was torture

not being able to touch. She only had me in her mouth for a minute earlier, but just the thought of those cherry lips around my dick has me harder than a fruitcake."

"Stop," Cyn hissed.

"What? She made me, too. She wants me here just as much as you."

"She was trying to resurrect *me*. She knew nothing about you."

"Boys, hang on," Emma interjected while she hurriedly replaced her panties.

"So does that mean I'll be forced to stay in the back while you get laid? Maybe I'll just leave, then." Cris took a few steps toward the door, still clothed in nothing but the tattoos covering his body.

Emma's heart leapt when she imagined Cris walking naked down the street. The cries and chaos his presence would conjure. What if the sheriff arrested him? What if Nicoli used the scandal to further manipulate and control her? What if they took Cyn away, too?

"No one is stopping you, brother." Cyn gestured to the front windows. Cris shrugged and strode to the door, shoulders swinging with swagger.

"Wait!"

Cris halted his stride and glanced over his shoulder. "Yeah?"

"You can't leave. Please," Emma begged.

Cris's brow rose in surprise. "Why not? You don't want me here."

"No, I do. I'm sorry I got so carried away. That was rude of me, but please, please stay."

"Emma?"

She spun around to face Cyn and placed her palms on her chest. "He's your brother, Cyn. We can't let him wander out there alone."

Cyn's eyes darkened. "So you want him to stay with us? With you?"

Emma frowned. She knew the real question he was asking. Cris hadn't exactly been subtle with his demands. If he stayed, she'd be expected to devote the same attention to him that she gave to Cyn.

"What's it going to be, Emma?" Cris called.

It was the first time he'd said her name, and as much as she didn't want to admit it, she couldn't deny the butterflies it stirred in her. Emma pivoted to face Cris and brushed the few flyaways out of her face. "I want you to stay."

# CHAPTER FIVE

A satisfied smirk split Cris's lips. "All right, now we're going to have a party." He jogged over to where they stood, wrapped his arms around Emma's waist, and twirled her around in the air.

An involuntary giggle slipped from her lips as she held onto his firm biceps. Cris set her down on her feet and kissed her forehead. Then his gaze shifted upward. "Chill out, Cyn. Nervous your girl is going to like my dick more?"

Cyn's eyes hardened. "We should get to work. Emma still has orders to fill." He spun away and retied his apron, marching into the back room without looking back.

"He's always been the serious one. Don't worry. I'll make sure you have a good time, honey cake." Cris pinched her nipple through her shirt, eliciting a high-pitched squeal.

"Hey!" Emma playfully swatted his hand and handed him an extra baker's coat. "Put this on."

Cris laughed and shrugged into its embrace. "Is my massive junk too distracting?"

"No. But I do prepare and serve food here. It'll be cleaner and safer around the ovens for you."

"Sure, sure." Cris smirked. "You can pretend to be a good girl, but from the size of this cock you gave me, I can tell you're horny as hell."

Emma's jaw dropped, but she didn't deny it. She hadn't been with anyone since Cyn. Jane had introduced her to guys, but all of them had lacked a certain spark when she'd looked at them. Not like Cyn, and surprisingly, not like Cris, either. He had a playful streak that bordered on aggression.

*I wonder how he'd fuck me.*

The thought wove into her mind before she could taper it. Heat flushed her cheeks and guilt squeezed her chest. She'd waited so long for Cyn to come back to her; it almost felt like cheating just envisioning tasting Cris's sweet cock again or him bending her over. The image changed and the three of them together exploded like a firework. What if the boys shared? Her sex clenched at the idea of the brothers fucking her at the same time. Hells. What had come over her? Emma could already feel herself getting wet at the mere possibility. Would Cyn go for it? Maybe if she asked nicely . . . with her lips wrapped around his cock.

A warm hand traced the gentle curve of her blouse and settled firmly against her throat, squeezing just enough to direct her attention toward a pair of dark irises inches from her own.

"Tell me." Cris's voice was low and rough. A command.

Emma blinked, her lashes fluttering against his jawline. "Tell you what?"

"What you want me to do to you. I see it in your eyes, the slight part of your lips." He groaned. "What I'd give to hear my name in your mouth while I pleasure you." His hand flexed, tightening. It sent a wave of heat rippling through her body. At her silence, he continued and dragged the tip of his nose along her cheekbone to the shell of her ear. "Crumbs, you smell so fine, like spun sugar. I can't wait to taste, but first, I need to try your gumdrops."

His hands roamed over the full hourglass curves of her waist up to her breasts. He palmed the slight swells through the thin cotton, cradling their weight as he bounced them. "You're beautiful, but I'm curious to learn more. Exactly what color are your little rosebuds under there?" He pinched both nipples, then lingered, pulling the peaks until Emma rewarded him with a low sigh.

Spurred on by her favorable reaction, Cris tugged her blouse open farther to reveal a triangle of smooth lightly freckled skin. The topmost button popped, followed by the second, and the material parted to her navel under Cris's touch. Emma swallowed roughly, causing her breasts to rise closer to him.

"Fuck. You're perfect." Cris leaned in and licked the skin of her neck, sprinkling hot kisses down to her collarbone.

Emma's head dropped back, and she released another sigh as goosebumps pebbled her skin. Cris's hand slipped beneath her shirt. Running the pad of his thumb over the lacy pattern of her bra and stiff nipple, he smiled.

"Does that feel good?" Cris's voice was hard as if he were restraining himself. The fact that he was fighting for control sent Emma's need into overdrive.

"Yes," she whispered. Her tongue ran along her lower lip while she leaned into his touch.

Dipping his fingers inside the material, Cris released her breast and cupped it in his hand, flicking the pink bud to draw a startled gasp from her. He moved closer. The chef's coat was long forgotten, puddled in a heap at their feet. Had he even put it on? His erection pressed against her leg, the crown straining toward the apex of her thighs, pawing at her skirt. Emma ached, clenching with desire.

Cris groaned. "So fucking lovely." He lowered his head, and his tongue darted between his lips. Emma could almost feel the heat of his mouth. It sent shivers down her spine. She wanted that mouth on her. She arched closer, a subtle hint.

At last, he licked, tongue warm and wet, but it wasn't enough as he teased her nipple. Snaking her arm up, Emma clasped the back of his neck to pull him closer. "Please," she urged.

"Are you two coming or what?" Cyn's head poked out from around the doorframe. There was no way to hide their actions, not with Emma's breast falling out of her bra and Cris nearly kneeling before her.

"Well, not anymore," Cris growled. He straightened

to his full height and pulled her bra back into place.

Coral color stained Emma's cheeks. She could feel the weight of Cyn's gaze. It was predatory, but something else brewed there. He looked away before she could identify it. She noted the way his jaw pulsed. He was clearly gritting his teeth. Her gut plummeted. She'd never meant to cause him pain, hadn't planned on any of this . . .

Cris bent down and scooped the white coat off the floor. He shrugged into it and with deft fingers, punched the buttons through. Emma caught sight of his erection softening and internally groaned.

"Couldn't have gotten started without us, huh?" Cris called. His broad shoulders swayed powerfully as he strode toward the back. Masculinity and sex appeal radiated off him like pheromones.

Cyn assessed his brother and frowned. Emma didn't miss the way his eyes lingered in her direction. He raised his hand and touched Cris's chest, stalling his momentum to whisper something too low for her to hear. Cris cocked his head and grinned, then wandered out of sight into the kitchen.

Emma's fingers flew to rebutton her blouse as she moved to Cyn's side. "What was that about?"

Cyn's heavy-lidded gaze wandered up and down her frame. "Just reminding him of a few things."

"Like?" Emma shook out her ruined braid and pulled it into a high ponytail.

"Like the fact that this sweet cunny is mine." Suddenly, Cyn's hand cupped her sex.

She moaned when he traced the outline of her through her panties. Emma closed her eyes, but when she opened them again, Cyn's frown had deepened. "What's wrong?"

"You're so wet, so ready."

"And?" Emma giggled. "What's the problem?"

"Did Cris make you this wet?"

Emma rolled her eyes and smacked his arm. "You both did." Her response didn't fix his scowl. "Come on. You're not being fair, here. I've been trying to make *you* for months. I didn't know if I'd ever see you again. And I especially didn't intend to make your brother, too. But now we're all here together, so stop ruining it. This is supposed to be a happy day. You're finally back." She closed the distance between them and kissed him softly. "You have no idea how much I've missed you."

Cyn wrapped both arms around her. He laid a soft kiss on her forehead. "You're right. I'm sorry. I have no right to act like this. It's just hard, seeing him touch you and you . . . responding the way you do, but—"

Emma felt tension in the way he held her. "What is it, Cyn?"

"I liked it."

"What? But I thought—"

Cyn shook his head. "Believe me, part of me hates seeing another man put his hands on you, but watching you? Hearing the way your breath changes. Seeing the way your body arches? It's a real fucking turn-on."

A wrinkle formed between Emma's brows. "You liked watching me with Cris?"

His gaze turned dark, smoldering her in place. "Yeah. You were so hot, so free. It was a whole new vantage point. How would you feel about it?"

"About what?"

"If I watched before joining in." Cyn's words hung in the air between them.

The relief that ballooned in Emma's chest was huge. "You want to watch your brother be intimate with me?"

"Only if you're okay with it. I know it will be different than our relationship before, and the idea of you being with someone else was infuriating at first, but once I saw the two of you together . . ." He shook his head. "I can't stop thinking about it."

Emma bit her lip. Voyeurism was never something she'd planned for, let alone participated in. Before Cyn, her sex life had consisted of the obligatory marital union once she'd become Henry's wife. The old pig had lasted barely a minute thrusting into her. After, he never tried to touch her again in a sexual manner. For that small mercy, she was grateful. Then, Cyn had magically appeared in her life and introduced her to a whole new world of happiness and pleasure. Never did she think she'd find love in this life or a partner willing to indulge her fantasies. If this was something Cyn wanted, she was open to trying.

Butterflies tickled her stomach, but beneath their papery wings was a much stronger carnal desire. All her life, she'd been nearly invisible. Now, she had the chance to be seen in an unexpected new light.

"Okay," Emma whispered.

"Are you sure?"

"Absolutely. You opened me to so many sexual experiences. If there's something I can do for you, I'm excited to make you happy." She pointed a flour-stained finger at him. "So long as you promise to join in at some point."

"Deal." In one swift motion, Cyn bent his knees and scooped her into his arms. Emma's legs went wide as she fought to secure herself around his hips. Her skirt rode up, and she was painfully aware of how soaked they'd made her.

"Fuck, sugarcane. Your heart is racing. You want these dicks, don't you?"

Emma sank lower in his arms and wiggled her hips. The top of Cyn's cock where it was tucked in the apron thickened under her light bounce. "Only every moment since you left me behind."

A crisp slap stung Emma's ass. Cyn chuckled at her yelp of surprise and captured her lips with his. "My apologies, love. I never meant to leave you." His voice grew serious, his eyes molten pools of sorrow.

Emma pulled back and traced the bow of his lip. "I know. You can't begin to understand how happy I am that I found you once more."

"No *once* this time. This time, it's forever. As long as you don't have another shotgun-wielding husband?"

Emma's first real laugh in years echoed around them. "No chance of that."

Cyn smacked her ass again, harder this time—a promise of more to come. "Let's get started, then."

# CHAPTER SIX

Cyn palmed her ass and spread her cheeks, baring her pussy. The thought of him carrying her over to where Cris waited and dropping her onto his stiff cock made her hips rock. She'd be just like a pretty dancer atop a peg in a music box, salaciously dancing while Cyn stood back and watched. Performing for him would be so erotic. It was one thing to make him cum while he was buried inside her, but the power to do the same by putting on a show was intoxicating. He sank two fingers inside her wetness, bringing her out of her naughty thoughts.

Emma moaned. "Not yet."

Cyn withdrew. "I'm sorry. I thought—"

"No, no, I want to. *Trust* me. But I really need to remake these orders first." Cyn groaned his displeasure. "At least let me get them in the oven."

A guttural rumble reverberated in Cyn's throat. "Fine. But the moment that oven door closes, you're riding Cris's cock. Got it?"

"Yes, sir." Emma smiled and pressed her breasts against his chest.

"Don't push it, sugar." He gave her a swift kiss and carefully released her, letting her slide down the front of him. He'd grown from thick to rock-hard during their conversation, and the bulge under his apron was impossible to miss.

"Come on, man," Cris called from around the corner. "If I can't play, neither can you." He pulled Emma across the threshold and twirled her in front of the main table. "Tell us what to do."

Cyn joined his brother and awaited instructions with a smile. They were both trying to behave like good boys. Emma wished they could skip to the part where they were dirty and depraved, but she did have a shop to run.

"Right. First, everyone wash your hands and put on some pants. There are extra in that box over there." Emma brushed aside a few curling tendrils from her face as she followed her own advice. Once everyone was clean and clothed to her liking, she said, "Cyn, grab some dough from the icebox. Cris, start spreading flour across the surface of the counter." She handed him a half-empty bag and a large metal scoop. Spinning in a tight circle, she located her mother's rolling pin and ran her fingers lovingly down the wood grain. Its magic had brought Cyn back after so much solitude.

The icebox door slammed, and Cyn hefted a wrapped parcel of dough into the air. "Do you need all of this?"

Emma waved her hands in a gesture to pass it to her. "Probably not. I only need two large cookies. I'm so glad I made double the amount of dough when it was slow yesterday. I guess I had a feeling I was going to need it."

"You mean because two hunky men were going to transform from your baked goods?" Cris laughed. He brushed his floury hands on the front of his coat, then collected the fallen trays. Without being told, he took them to the deep sink and got to work washing them.

Her carefree chuckle warmed the room. "Yes, deep down, I knew you'd be coming today."

"One can only hope." Cris glanced over his shoulder and winked.

Emma gasped and hit him playfully on the arm. With his bulging muscles, she doubted he could even feel it.

The sound of crinkling paper chittered as Cyn unwrapped the dough. "Should I just pull this apart?"

"Here, let me." Emma grabbed a long knife and expertly sliced through the roll of chilled dough, separating the amount necessary for each order.

"Remind me not to get on your bad side," Cyn teased as his eyes followed the precise cuts of the blade.

Emma arched her brow. "You intimidated?"

"Absolutely."

"Good. I've got lots of skills you don't even know about."

Cyn grinned. "Oh really? Enlighten me."

Taking the smaller amount of sliced dough, Emma rolled it through the sprinkled flour, kneading and warming it until it became just the right temperature to roll out. "Well, when I was little, I could climb any tree no matter how high. I used to get to the highest branch possible and pretend I was a bird, humming and whistling while I watched the world below."

"Did you ever fall?"

"I slipped once but caught myself before I got too banged up. I had a few bruises."

"Too banged up?" Cris repeated. "Ain't no such thing."

Emma leveled a smirk in Cris's direction. "There is when you're thirty feet in the air with nothing to catch you."

"Oh, I'd catch you. There's no falling with me. Unless it's onto a bench so I can have my way with you." Cris purred behind his teeth. Emma could feel the vibration in her own chest.

"A bench? Don't you mean a bed?"

His hearty laugh echoed in the shared space. "Damn. Seems I've got a few things to teach you that even my brother doesn't know."

"Or maybe I respect women too much to subject them to the depraved acts you view as romantic," Cyn argued.

"It's not depraved if they ask me to go harder." Cris offered a large goofy grin.

"You're incorrigible."

"Don't be mad your girl missed out because you're too vanilla."

Emma's face flushed while her thoughts pulled back to that amazing day with Cyn. The way he'd instructed her how to take his length in her mouth and relax her throat to take him even deeper. How he'd chased her around the house and cum on her breasts, marking her as his. Then laid her down and made her orgasm with just his tongue. And after, when he'd bent her over the counter and fucked her while spanking her ass. Every single one of those acts had blown her mind and completely overshadowed her inexperience with lovemaking. Yet, Cris was calling Cyn vanilla? What else could there possibly be? Just the memory of Cyn's thick cock made her clench with need. Damn these gingerbread orders.

"What exactly do you do with a bench?" Emma kept her eyes trained on the dough growing stickier between her fingers. She tried to keep her voice neutral but even she heard the way her breath hitched at the end. Suddenly, a warm presence enveloped her, and two rough hands roamed over her hips, tugging at her blouse. Cris's deep timbre kissed her ear. Shivers licked her spine. How she wanted him to dive under the fabric and touch her . . .

"A bed is so limiting. It can't offer optimal positioning for penetration. It's too soft. A bench . . ." He nipped her neck. "It has far more support so I can bend you over on your knees and make you bounce on my dick. It's so much deeper, honey cake." His fingers brushed the front of her panties. "Let me pleasure you, Emma."

Cris's voice was intoxicating, lulling her into a trance. The dough hardened under her nails. If she didn't roll it out now, she'd sacrifice the texture, and the cookie wouldn't bake properly.

Stepping out from under his touch, Emma knocked into him with her hip to gain some distance. "Maybe later. We need to focus now. Grab me that cutter on the second shelf." She pinched the fine flour and tossed it in Cris's face.

The powder stuck to his jaw and his lips. "You did not just do that."

Emma cocked her head. "And what if I did?"

"Oh, honey cake, the things I'm going to do to punish you for that naughty behavior." Cris's eyes burned. He wasn't joking. Emma's thighs tingled with anticipation.

Cyn gave his brother a shove toward the shelf. "Time for all that later, lover boy. The faster we get these done, the more time for extracurriculars." He scooped a generous amount of flour onto the crinkling dough tangled in Emma's fingers. "There. Now we can massage this back into shape." He stepped behind her, and together, they kneaded the pile again, soothing the cracks that had formed, careful to keep a maddening breadth of space between them. When a firm sphere had resulted, he handed her the fateful rolling pin. "Why don't you do the honors?"

A challenging smirk pulled at the corner of Emma's mouth. "What if I unknowingly create more gingerbread men?"

Cyn shook his head and kissed the top of hers. "It'd be a shame for them because I refuse to share you with anyone else. Besides, it wasn't the rolling pin, but your tears associated with its destruction that called me back to life to comfort you."

Emma leaned back against his chest and tilted her chin up to look at him. His chiseled jaw met her gaze. Wisps of a tattoo traced the defined line. "I know how you can comfort me."

Cyn smoothed the dough and took the rolling pin from her hands. "Now who's being naughty? I feel like a parent around you two."

"Does that mean I should call you Daddy?" Emma arched her ass.

A groan built behind Cyn's teeth. "No, that's never been a kink for me, but I do like, *sir*."

"Sir Cyn. I like that."

"Just as long as you know I'm not a knight in shining armor come to rescue you. Think of me as your boss, making you carry out my every whim."

"Deal." Emma reached onto her toes and captured Cyn's lips. His tongue flicked out, and the taste of cinnamon made her lips buzz. She slid her arm up and brought him closer, trying to deepen the kiss, but he reared back and clucked his tongue.

"So naughty." A crisp spank made her yelp. "Get back to work."

"Yes, sir." Emma winked and pressed down on the rolling pin, wiggling her ass.

"Not gonna work, sugar."

Emma replied with a playful pout but turned her attention back to the dough at hand. The trio worked in silence for a short while, and the sounds of baking filled the small kitchen. A low hum warmed her throat, and a simple tune swelled forth. A few minutes later, the front bell chimed, announcing a customer.

"Want me to get it?" Cris asked.

Emma frowned. "And worry about you flashing your junk to some poor unsuspecting person? No thanks." She leveled him with a pointed stare. "Stay."

Cris snickered. "That's fair."

Emma rolled her eyes and left the kitchen. Her friend Jane stood waiting, half-distorted by the display case's curved glass. "Hey, stranger. How are you today?" Emma turned on the small sink and lathered her hands before rinsing the bubbles away.

Jane sighed and gestured to the case. "Is it just me or are your cookies' appendages getting bigger?"

"Well, what do you expect from a widow?"

Jane snorted. "You mean since your mystery man disappeared? We both know Henry couldn't inspire *this* kind of artwork."

"I never should have told you." Emma laughed.

"But you had to so that I, being your best friend, could steer you toward a man that actually exists."

"We've been over this."

"Oh, come on, Em. The men in this town aren't all bad."

Emma raised a brow. "Name one decent single guy."

Jane stuck her hands on her hips. "Calvin."

"With the scaly scalp condition?"

"What about George?"

"Bleh. He's so self-absorbed."

Jane frowned. "Alan?"

"Ew, Jane he *just* turned eighteen."

Jane threw up her hands and made an exasperated noise. "You are so picky."

"No. I know what I want and refuse to settle for less, especially now that Henry's gone and I can go after what and who I want."

Jane took a step back and furrowed her brow, assessing her. "Something's happened."

"What do you mean?"

"You're so much more . . . I don't know, alive and vibrant. Did you get some?"

"You would know if I had."

A slow smile spread on Jane's lips as she shook her head back and forth. "Not if it just happened."

Damn, she was quick. Emma bit her lip, preparing to deny Jane's claim when her friend's eyes flared wide and her mouth formed an elongated 'O.'

"He's back, isn't he?" Jane squealed.

"Well—"

Jane's hands flew to her face. "He's here? Like *right* now?"

"How did you—"

"Oh please, it's all over your face!" Jane waved her hands. "You've always been such a terrible liar. So did you do it yet?"

"Jane, I'm working." Emma lowered her voice, a subtle cue for her friend to do the same.

"In other words, you're not busy, but you want to be!" Jane wiggled her eyebrows along with her hips.

"Believe it or not, I do have orders to fill before anything else can commence. Now, do you want to grab something or not?"

"Geez, pushy," Jane said. "But yes. As a fellow spinster who needs to get laid, give me two regular gingerbread men with marshmallow-iced cocks."

Emma bent down and slid open the back of the case. Her cheeks burned as the truth of her situation fully hit her. *She* had two gingerbread men waiting to fuck her. Cyn had even asked if he could watch. Dozens of nights, she and Jane had stayed up late commiserating over their hopeless love lives in the remote Pennsylvania town, swallowing glass after glass of wine as if the answer to their strife lay at the bottom of the tented bottle. Turns out, the secret was actually contained in a more useful tool.

After withdrawing two cookies from the shelf, Emma loaded them into a paper bag and punched in the total. "That'll be seventy-five cents."

A crisp snap came from Jane's coin purse as its silver mouth yawned wide. She pulled the proper coins from the sagging depths and slid them across the countertop.

"Thank you." Emma plunked the money into the belly of the register. "Have a nice evening, Jane."

Her friend's fingers crinkled the lip of the bag with a knowing smile. "Don't be afraid to send that lover of yours my way when you're done with him."

They were great friends, but the idea of sharing Cyn with anyone brought up an acidic taste in the back of her throat. Now she understood his reaction to Cris's demand. "I wouldn't hold your breath," Emma said with a hard smirk.

Jane pouted. "You need to learn how to share."

She winked and blew Emma a kiss before pivoting in her boots and sashaying out the door. The bell chimed again to announce her exit, and Emma released a relieved sigh. Unknowingly, that had been her first test. How would her life continue now that Cyn had returned? As long as Henry didn't come back from the dead and riddle Cyn with bullets, there was nothing to endanger him this time.

She imagined picking up where they'd left off two years ago. Fleeing Henry's oppressive house, they'd have run past the next town and the next until they found one that felt right. There, they could have crafted a home perfect for them, complete with a large kitchen of course, and settled into a life of love, getting lost in one another's touch and exploring new ways to pleasure. Maybe even a child or two if Cyn was capable of such magic. Now that he'd returned, could such a future become reality?

A sour pit formed in her stomach as Nicoli's smug expression filtered into her thoughts. What would become of her now that he'd materialized? The police hadn't looked twice when Emma had run to them after Henry's death, tears carving her face. They'd believed her story of his suicide easily. In their small town, everyone knew her husband had a temper and often acted rashly when he was inebriated. They didn't have special blood splatter teams or forensics to analyze the scene. Emma's account, along with her reserved and quiet demeanor, was all the evidence they'd needed. No one suspected she was the one who'd pulled the trigger.

She hadn't meant to kill Henry. Her only thought had been to save Cyn from his rage, but she couldn't deny that she wasn't disappointed with the outcome. The police hadn't suspected her, but perhaps Nicoli did and his appearance was a combination of greed and blackmail. The sooner she figured out a way to cleanse him from her life, the better.

# CHAPTER SEVEN

Emma's hands twisted in her apron, her anxiety somewhat calmed by the friction the starched cloth created. She drifted toward the front windows and peered into the darkening sky. The clock ticked closer to five—closing time—and with each second, the sun edged closer to the horizon, taking its warmth with it.

A shiver snaked up her spine and Emma abandoned the apron's pockets and wrapped her arms around her torso instead. Several people milled about on the sidewalk, finishing the last of their errands before shopkeepers closed up for the day.

On the opposite side of the street, an elderly couple held hands, their wrinkled skin fitting perfectly together after years of proximity. Would that ever be her one day? If Cyn stayed this time, would he age or would his magic keep him young forever while she became gnarled and gray?

Her breath fogged up the glass in a clinging white cloud. The vapor cloaked the sweet scene from view. A melancholy sigh slipped from Emma's lips, and she rested her forehead on the cool surface. Warm hands slid around her waist and pulled her back against a solid body.

"What are you doing out here?" Cyn's deep voice was soft, curious.

Emma sank into his embrace and pointed toward the couple. "Watching them."

"Them?" Cyn's surprise was evident. "Are they friends of yours?"

Emma shook her head. "No, but they got me thinking. Do you age? Can we grow old together? Do you even want to?" Her voice was small, and she bowed her head to avoid Cyn's questioning gaze.

He was quiet for a minute. Emma held her breath as he massaged small circles into her lower back. "Of course, I want to grow old with you, but . . . the truth is, I don't know what's going to happen. Last time, our experience was cut short. I don't have a magic timer or an expiration date. All I want is to stay with you, but I don't want to make you a promise I can't keep."

The weight of Cyn's words speared harder than they should have. Hadn't she just been contemplating the same thing? But to hear him agree and share the same doubts cemented that the chance they'd be able to create something more solid than a few glorious hours of lovemaking was slim. The magic would expire at some point, and Emma would be alone again. A broken sob erupted from her chest. Cyn's arms tightened around her in a heartbeat.

"I'm so sorry, sugarcane. Believe me, I will do

everything in my power to stay with you as long as possible." Cyn kissed her temple and turned her gently to face him. Using the pad of his thumb, he traced the curve of her cheekbone and stole her tears. "Please don't cry. Let's enjoy every moment we do have."

Emma nodded, pressed his palm harder against her face, and planted a soft kiss on the heel of his hand. "You're right. We can't change the future. Who knows what might happen, right?"

Mirth lit Cyn's gaze. "Exactly, though I can tell you with certainty what I *do* have planned for you."

Heat rushed into Emma's cheeks as Cyn's hold turned from protective to predatory.

"Cyn . . ." She sighed when his hands roamed to the front of her shirt and dipped into the open valley between the buttons. His long fingers grazed the swell of her breasts. Slowly, he peeled back the material to expose her bra beneath.

"You're so beautiful." Cyn forced the fabric wider. One of the buttons gave way, unable to withstand his search when his touch roughened. With both hands, he yanked her bra down, spilling her breasts over the underwire. Her nipples peaked, exposed to the cold air as well as the heat coming off her gingerbread man.

Emma sucked in a sharp breath and hunched her shoulders to cover herself in front of the large window. "Someone will see."

Cyn cupped her right breast and bounced it in his palm. "Good. They should see what perfection looks like." He slid his hand and pinched her nipple, rolling it between his fingers until he drew a breathy groan from her. Then he replaced his touch with his hot mouth, continuing to tease and nip her flesh with his tongue.

Emma's head fell back as pleasure gripped her in a powerful wave. "Cyn," she moaned, growing desperate. Still, she angled her body farther away from the window to shield her nudity from the street.

A firm hand gripped her waist. When she found Cyn's gaze again, hot coals burned in his eyes. "I thought I told you never to cover these in my presence?" His voice was so deep, possessed of carnal energy.

"But the window—"

"I told you, let them see. Let them all know you're mine." His growl was feral, and his peppermint breath made her sensitive skin prickle with desire. "I doubt they'd be able to see much anyway, sugar. Take a look."

Directing her hips, Cyn spun her to face the front faster than she could protest. A cloudy wall met her frightened gaze. The street and her reflection were gone, the glass painted with their labored breaths instead. Emma couldn't see out, so no one could peer inside either, their activities cloaked by a curtain of steam.

"Did you turn the oven on?" Emma asked.

"Sure did. Cris and I finished rolling out both orders and popped them in."

"How did you know the right temperature? You didn't guess, did you?"

Cyn fixed her with an incredulous look and gestured down the length of him. "I think I know the perfect temp to make a cookie come out good and hard. And before you ask, Cris set the timer and will pull them out when they're ready."

Emma arched her eyebrows. "Thanks, but I'm not sure I like this talk about pulling out. You sure you know what you're doing?" Emboldened by the opaque windows, she spread her legs. Hitching one over his hip, she dragged her skirt slowly up her thigh until her panties peeked out.

Cyn groaned through gritted teeth and straightened, both hands falling to her waist. "Then again, I suppose you're the expert. Just one touch and look at what you do to me." He yanked down his waistband and unbuttoned the last clasp on his baker's jacket. His dark cock sprang forward, seeking Emma's warmth. Her moan caused his length to twitch against her thigh. Cyn grasped his shaft and pumped, palming the glistening crown before he guided his hand to the base.

Emma's eyes widened. Hells, it was definitely bigger. The memory of choking around his cock assailed her. She'd never be able to take all of him this time. Cyn guided the tip toward her and rubbed it along her soft mound. Her panties were drenched; she was so eager for him.

"Do you want me, sugar?"

"More than anything." Emma ground her pussy against his crown, desperate for friction.

"Fuck, you *are* ready."

Emma nodded and licked her lips. Was she really about to fuck her gingerbread man on full display of the street with nothing but faith in a foggy window to protect her decency? Abso-fucking-lutely.

"I want you to show me," Cyn ordered.

Emma nudged the fabric to the side, baring her wet cunny to him. With her other hand, she pulled his cock closer and dragged the head against her clit. Cyn exhaled when the crown of his cock shone with her arousal.

"Damn, that's so hot, but I want you to do something else first."

The desire to sink onto his shaft was driving Emma mad. "You mean . . ." With a slight tilt of her head, she lined him up with her entrance and pushed down just slightly to envelope the tip. ". . . you want me to stop? You don't want to grab my hips and slam me onto you again and again?" Her voice was breathy, and her breasts heaved with need.

Cyn threw his head to the side and cursed. "Not yet, sugar. The buildup is my favorite part." He took a slight step back, and his cock slipped out of her center.

A pout transformed Emma's vixen-like pose. "How else would you like me to show you how much I want you, then . . . sir?" She didn't miss the way his cock pulsed when she addressed him with the formal title. That small amount of power felt good. Just her words made him thick.

"Take me in your mouth. You remember what I taught you, right?" Cyn grinned as if in challenge.

Emma pursed her lips. "Be warned, I haven't had any practice. I'm a little rusty."

"You didn't hesitate to take my brother in your mouth earlier."

Emma's brow ticked up. "Oh, jealous, are we?"

Cyn's touch hardened and his fingers buried into the skin of her waist. "I was, but I can't get the image of your lips wrapped around his dick out of my mind. Before you take him, show me you're mine. Show me you want *me* too, sugarcane." Before Emma could reply, Cyn forced her to her knees and thrust his cock between her lips.

Her tongue cradled the underside of his shaft. The flavors of cinnamon, vanilla, and marshmallow abounded in her mouth. Emma's thighs clenched involuntarily. Yes, he was definitely bigger.

"Eyes on me," Cyn said. Emma placed one hand on Cyn's stomach while she cradled his balls with her other. "Fuck, sugar." He brushed wisps of hair out of her face and clutched her ponytail, silently urging her to take him deeper. "Show me you're mine."

The demand shot straight to her sex. Emma gave his balls one more squeeze, then dropped her hand to her lap. She relaxed her throat and bobbed her head, ushering his length farther and farther into her mouth until his cock hit the back of her throat. She gagged slightly but breathed through it, her eyes never leaving his. If Cyn needed reassurance, she could certainly give him that.

"Fuck, fuck, fuck," Cyn said through clenched teeth as he thrust deeper into her mouth, his hips following the rhythm and pace she set.

Emma pulled back and ran her tongue along the underside, up and down the sides, then sucked on the crown with vigor before swallowing his entire girth as far as she could once more.

"Damn," Cyn drawled when his head fell to the side. "Do that again."

"Yes, sir." Emma fluttered her lashes. This time, her tongue traced the frosted tattoos she'd piped earlier, including the little smudge she'd accidentally made with her nail. He'd come to life before she could fix it. Cyn swelled beneath her touch. She'd make him cum, but she wanted to climax with him too.

Rolling her hips, Emma slipped her hand between her legs and dipped two fingers inside her wetness while her thumb ground against her clit. She moaned around Cyn's cock as he thrust into her mouth.

"Shit, sugar, are you touching yourself? I love it when you do that," Cyn said. "Your mouth feels so fucking good, and you're fucking tongue . . ." He groaned. He was so close. Luckily, so was she. All their teasing from earlier had left her on the cusp of an orgasm, and her skillful fingers, along with the knowledge that she was about to make Cyn cum, propelled her toward the precipice. The high was building inside her, threatening to crest as she took Cyn's cock in her mouth once more, working it until he moaned.

"Sugar . . . I can't."

Emma pulled back, circling her clit faster. "Then give it to me, Cyn." Still looking up at him through her lashes, she stuck out her pink tongue in invitation.

"Shit," Cyn groaned. Grabbing his shaft, he slapped the crown of his cock atop the smooth surface and exploded with warm marshmallow cum. The sweet flavor flowed over her tongue and lips as her own climax built. She was so close, so ready to tip over the edge.

Two hands slid beneath her breasts and jerked her backward, dislodging her hand and tearing her orgasm away.

"If you think I'm going to let you cum around your own hand, you're in for a very long night, honey cake." Cris's dark molten eyes bored into her own before he picked her up and stole her away from Cyn's cock.

# CHAPTER EIGHT

"Cris, no!" Emma whined when the delicious tension instantly diminished as her focus was ripped away. "You're ruining it."

Cris scoffed and cradled her against his chest. "No, love. I promise to make it so much better. How could you do that to her?" His words were accusatory as he directed his hard stare toward his brother.

"You don't understand," Cyn started. His cock was still thick and dripped marshmallow cream.

"Let me guess, she prefers to get you off?" Cris rolled his eyes.

"It's about anticipation, brother." Cyn's words were hard like a stale cookie threatening to snap.

"Hmm, well that doesn't work for me. I prefer to make my lovers cum as many times as they possibly can."

"Cris, he's telling the truth. We take care of each other—"

Cris kissed her full on the mouth, effectively cutting off her explanation. In a low voice, he whispered in her ear. "I know, love, but I never learned how to share either, and I want to taste that sweet orgasm of yours first."

"But—" Emma tried to reason with him, but between his frenzied movements and Cyn's murderous glare, she doubted the other gingerbread man would hear her anyway.

Without setting her down, Cris lit the tall candles arranged along the far wall and those on the small coffee table situated in front of the love seat where patrons could dine in if they chose. On the opposite side of the room, he extinguished the thicker candles she'd lit earlier, the same ones that illuminated Cyn's position, casting him in inky shadow. One more remained flickering over the display case, a night light for her little cookies. To anyone not inside, the bakery appeared closed.

"What are you doing?" Emma asked, still caged tightly in Cris's arms.

"Setting the proper mood. Did you think I was going to give you the best climaxes of your life kneeling on the dirty floor?" He snickered under his breath and threw another glance in Cyn's direction, but it was too dark to see her lover's expression.

"And you thought you could just steal her from me without repercussions?" Cyn's gruff question wove out of the darkness. He took a step forward, and the nearby flame highlighted half his face, his scowl.

Emma's sex clenched. He looked dangerous; it was the same threatening look he'd given Henry. Before, she'd been too terrified to appreciate the way his steeled jaw punctuated his chiseled cheekbones, his brow heavy with power. Damn, he looked good.

"Don't think of it as stealing, brother. Besides, it's about the anticipation, remember? What better way to foster tension than by watching her ride my tongue, then my fingers, and my cock? Though I'm not decided on that order yet."

Emma shot a worried glance at Cyn. While she couldn't deny how Cris's words affected her, would being intimate with Cris harm their relationship? Cyn did say he wanted to watch. Did that wish still apply now that his brother was putting it to the test, though?

A moment of tense silence bloomed between the trio. Then, with the slightest inclination of his chin, Cyn took a step back and slid into one of the overstuffed armchairs—a silent granting of permission. His face was once more cloaked in darkness, but the hard planes of his chest were visible, along with his swirling tattoos. The candlelight also shone on his cock and his hand wrapped around the base. Slowly, he pumped his shaft. He needed a little time to get hard again after cumming on her tongue. Hells. The image of him in that chair was so erotic, and they hadn't even started yet.

"Excellent," Cris purred against Emma's neck. In the next breath, she was cocooned in a rush of cold air as his deft fingers expertly rid her of every button, clasp, hook, and string until she was standing completely nude before him. Her hands automatically slapped at her nakedness. "None of that," Cris reprimanded with a light slap on her ass.

"But you haven't even locked the door!" He reached behind him. The solid bolt clicked into place and calmed her racing heart somewhat. "They can still see. You lit candles right in front of me!"

Cris shook his head. "With all the heavy breathing I'm about to make you do, there's no chance anyone will see anything, love. Like when the oven produces heat and clouds the little glass window."

Emma opened her mouth to protest, but Cris grabbed her by the waist and with a swift flip, maneuvered her through the air. Instead of landing on her feet, her knees hit the firm sofa cushions, and her hands met the same material. A surprised huff of air escaped from Emma's lips but morphed into a deep moan as Cris sat behind her and plunged his tongue into her slit.

"Fuck!" Emma's hands turned to claws and raked the worn fabric. His tongue was so warm and wet. Cris reared back and flattened his tongue, then proceeded to lick from bottom to top.

Heat and more heat enveloped her, and she sank into the sensation. Emma dropped her head and arched her ass higher. Cris immediately responded, gripping her hips to slam her pussy onto his face. He was buried in her cunt, tongue swirling, flicking, vibrating impossibly fast over her clit at an almost punishing pace. And the groans he made, as if she were the most decadent meal he'd ever tasted . . . Faster and faster, she rolled her hips, his tongue never ceasing its hypnotic thrumming while she ground against him, seeking that friction that only his cock could provide.

"Please, Cris." Emma uttered his name without thought. It rolled off her tongue as easily as Cyn's, the syllables sharp instead of soft. Would that upset him? Carefully, she peeked toward the dark alcove where Cyn sat. But instead of the furrowed brow or stern scowl she anticipated, Cyn was breathing hard while his cock swelled under his hand.

The fact that he was truly enjoying spectating sent another thrill through her core and made her ache to be filled. Cris lapped at her center and spread her ass cheeks. This time, he dragged his tongue higher, rimming her ass. At first, Emma flinched. No one had ever touched her there, but she was shocked to find herself leaning into Cris's touch, eager for more.

"Does my dirty girl like that?" Cris asked.

Emma nodded and sank lower into the couch so that her face now rested on the cushion. "Yes. Touch me again."

Cris's tongue performed magic, licking her from clit to ass. His teeth left little bites along the way, hard enough to mark her. A giggle slipped from her lips when she envisioned each bite manifesting in the shape of a gumdrop or snowflake—special symbols as unique as the man bestowing them.

"Am I boring you?" Cris's baritone rumbled.

"No—"

"Obviously, I'm not doing enough if you're making those kinds of sounds. You should be moaning, praising my name."

"I was only thinking—"

"That's the problem. I want to make you so delirious with pleasure that you can't even form words." Cris pulled away, but a firm hand moved from her hip to the back of her head, keeping her in the submissive position.

"You were, but—"

"Brace yourself," Cyn growled, his harsh command almost unrecognizable.

"I wasn't—" Emma tried to explain, but before she could utter another word, warmth speared her pussy, forcing her to take every agonizingly thick inch. "Holy fuck!" She groaned as she wrapped around Cris's girth. He didn't go slow or try to be gentle. Instead, he pounded his cock into her slit without giving her the chance to acclimate to his size. She was just supposed to withstand it. "Shit! What is wrong with you gingerbread boys?" Her words were strained, as she was barely able to breathe around the furious thrusts. Cris drove his cock in again and again. At first, it was nearly impossible to take all of him. His cock wasn't as long as Cyn's, but it was far thicker. She had to stretch around him, but after a few times, he slid right in.

"There we go. I knew you could take me," Cris praised her. "Do you like this big dick? Does it feel good?"

"I . . . ah . . . yes," Emma whined, falling into a rhythm.

"Good girl. Those are the sounds I want to hear. Fuck, this little cunny is so tight. Squeezing my dick like a vise. But I want more. I told you I was a greedy boy." Sliding his hand from the back of her head to her neck, Cris picked Emma off the couch and yanked her against his torso with savage ferocity. His cock slid free with the new angle.

"Put it back in," Emma begged, pressing her ass against his heat. She spread her knees to invite him back.

"Oh, I plan to, honey. But I'm beginning to enjoy this idea of 'building the anticipation.' What do you think, brother? Ready to jump in yet?"

Cyn crossed the lobby in an instant and rooted himself beside the couch. His shaft throbbed, near the length of her rolling pin. With their respective heights, he would only have to shift a few inches, and she could kiss the tip of his cock.

"Cyn," Emma whispered, reaching for him. He obliged and stepped closer. Guiding his cock, he traced the swell of her breasts with the tip and bounced the weight of it on her peaked nipples. "Fuck," she moaned and sank back into Cris's cock. The heat of him pressed against her ass while he teased her, keeping away from her dripping center on purpose.

"I want to taste your gumdrops, baby," Cris said. "Turn this way." His command was accompanied by a swift tug on her hips, and she swiveled to the left.

In sync, Cris and Cyn bent their heads and placed warm ovens of heat over each nipple, sucking her into their mouths. Cris licked while Cyn bit, each rolling a puckered bud between their lips and teeth. Their hands wandered down her torso and diverged. Cyn slid two fingers into her pussy, while his thumb dominated her clit, swirling in fast circles until she bucked under the pressure.

Cris on the other hand, went around the back, palming her ass and smacking it with crisp spanks. Each one caused Emma to curl forward, the pleasure so intense at the combined sensations. Had they done this before? Maybe she wasn't the first lonely woman to conjure up their magic. The notion should have filled her with insecurity, but she was too overcome with need.

Cyn's revolutions intensified, his fingers driving harder into her cunt as his thumb performed a magnificent solo on her swollen clit. She needed to be filled, to be stuffed to the absolute brim.

Cyn abandoned her breasts first, but not before giving her one last love bite. He straightened, and Cris smacked the flesh where Cyn's mouth had suckled seconds prior. Gripping his shaft, Cyn grabbed Emma's chin. "Open your mouth and stick out your tongue." His voice was so rough. She obeyed without question. The weight of his cock bounced onto the slick surface of her tongue. She gazed at him. He inhaled sharply and swore under his breath. "Fuck, those eyes, sugar. The things you fucking do to me."

Without breaking eye contact, Emma moaned and fit her lips over Cyn's length, drawing him halfway into her mouth. She wanted to make up for earlier and finish what she'd started properly before Cris tore her away. With demure licks and kisses, she coaxed groan after groan out of him, delighting when his cock pulsed and throbbed in response.

"You're so good at that. You're driving me wild." Cyn pulled her hair tie out. Curtains of golden hair tumbled past her shoulders and framed her face like a halo. "Beautiful." He swept the long tendrils to one side in a gentle caress. Then his hold turned animalistic as he wound her hair about his knuckles. "Open wide, sugar."

Emma tilted her head back just before Cyn drove his length behind her teeth. Her eyes flared as the crown of his cock hit the back of her throat. The impulse to gag seized her until Cyn started to move his hips and released some of the pressure. But the reprieve was short-lived. Using his firm hold on her hair, he thrust into her mouth and forced her head toward him. Again and again, Emma choked as his cock drilled into her throat.

Her nipples ached under the constant attention from Cris as he sucked and played with each one. Cyn's other hand never paused strumming her clit either. Both of them built and teased her orgasm out of her with finesse that bordered on cruelty. Somehow, they could tell each time she was close. Then they'd still their touches just long enough to delay her release and restrict satisfaction. No one had told her sexual torture would be in store.

Emma arched back into Cris harder, nearly balancing on his dick. The tip nudged her entrance as she was forced to swallow Cyn's shaft. Cris whistled low. "Damn, look how well she takes that cock. Girl could swallow a whole candy cane." He reached up and gently smacked her cheek. Cyn groaned. "Do you like how we play with you, honey cake? Do you like being our pretty little whore?"

Emma couldn't speak and instead responded with a moan in the back of her throat. She pushed back again, her cunt kissing Cris's crown. She tried to sink lower, to placate the desire demanding to be sated, but Cyn gripped her hair harder and pulled her mouth nearly flush against him, burying his full length down her throat. She couldn't breathe, couldn't pull away, couldn't escape the heat—not that she wanted to.

A guttural groan reverberated in Cyn's chest as he held her there, forcing her to submit. "Is this cock not enough for you, sugar? Do you need more?" He wrenched her back, and his shaft slipped free, glistening with her saliva. Emma gasped a large breath. "What do you think, Cris? Should we give this dirty girl what she wants?" Cyn pumped his throbbing cock. He bounced its heavy weight on her breasts, then tapped it against her cheeks. She parted her lips to wrap around him once more, but he dodged her attempts.

Emma furrowed her brows. Fine, if he didn't want to play fair . . . Reaching forward, she tried to grab his length with both hands, but Cris anticipated her rebellion and wrenched both of her arms behind her back in a powerful grip.

"Hey!" Emma exclaimed.

"Oh, does that make our little pastry mad? Are you not into bondage?" Cris laughed and tightened his hold.

Emma wrestled her shoulders, trying to break free, fully aware of how the movement made her tits heave and sway. Cyn's dark eyes were nearly black, pupils blown wide with lust. He palmed the tip of his cock again and dragged the precum down her lips. She tossed her long hair and fixed the haughty gingerbread man with a pointed look. "It's not the bondage I dislike but the way the pair of you continue to torment me. It's not fair."

"If you haven't noticed, honey cake, I haven't gotten a release yet. Trust me. I plan to fill that tight cunt and make you scream my name," Cris promised.

Emma's frown deepened. "Liar. You enjoy teasing me too much. Maybe you're scared you can't make me cum—"

Before she could finish her sentence, Cris growled, the sound gravelly and feral. With her hands still held behind her, he sank onto the cushion and pulled her down with him, right onto his cock.

Emma cried out, taken aback by the sudden pressure, but her shock didn't last for more than a few seconds before lust overwhelmed her and her body moved on instinct. At last, here was the friction she'd been desperate for. Cris's thick cock spread her while he thrust his hips to meet her.

"Fuck! Yes, Cris! Yes!" She bounced up and down his length, setting their pace. This time, he let her. Warm calloused hands released her arms and slipped to her hips, and he slammed her down harder. Emma slowed her pace and hovered just below the tip, then rolled her hips and drove down with the intensity Cris demanded. His head fell back, and he squeezed her ass.

"Fuck me, brother. This girl is fucking magic." Cris's voice strained, and he exhaled through clenched teeth. "I'm not going to last much longer. Do it."

Emma's eyes fluttered as she rode her own cresting wave. "Do what?"

Cyn was there to answer her question. Without a word, he gripped her chin once more and drove his cock back into her mouth. She delighted at the taste of him, warm marshmallow sliding over her tongue. He pumped into her even harder than before, as if mounting her was a competition between the two brothers. The thought of them fighting to be the one to please her most was thrilling. Quickly, she adjusted her pace to accommodate them both, stroking Cyn's shaft with her tongue while she rode Cris as roughly as she could. From the bite of his nails into her waist, to the way her roots burned from Cyn's hold, to the double penetration, Emma couldn't imagine sexual bliss got much better than this. She was so gloriously full, stuffed by two incredible men who were only interested in giving her pleasure.

"Emma," Cyn moaned. "Fuck, sugar. The way you suck me off. I'm so close."

Cyn's praise increased her tempo. Her own orgasm wasn't far behind his. Never had she been challenged like this, and all their stimulation skyrocketed her climax. Harder, she drove her pussy onto Cris's cock, taking all of it to the hilt. Her thighs burned, along with her abs, but she didn't slow. Her orgasm ignited, growing brighter and brighter with a ferocity she'd never experienced. Emma's clit thrummed and her G-spot pulsed into overdrive as Cris's cock hit the perfect spot. She was flying, soaring, her mind lost in an out-of-body experience as she reached the highest point. Squeezing Cyn's thigh, she signaled she was ready so they could cum together.

Behind her, Cris continued to grip her hips. Emma shot a look over her shoulder, and a thrill of power sparked. Cris's eyes were locked onto her body, hypnotized by the kinky slip of skin as her pussy glided along his shaft each time she rose higher on his length. He was a man possessed, obsessed. The thought sent a delicious shiver up her frame. Cyn's tightening grip brought her back to the present, back to the gingerbread man fucking her mouth.

"Fuck, fuck, fuck, Emma." With her hair gathered around his knuckles, Cyn held her head steady, forcing his entire length deep into her throat. "Right there, sugar. Stay right there and take this dick like a good girl."

His words sent her over the edge, and her climax imploded one second before his. Ribbons of pleasure radiated from Emma's center, sending tingling waves through her whole frame. At the same time, Cyn orgasmed ropes of warm marshmallow-flavored cum over her tongue. He tasted divine, a shot of gooey cream. She swallowed easily and gave him a satisfied smile.

Cyn withdrew his spent dick and traced Emma's lipstick-smeared mouth with the still dripping tip. She kissed him and ran her tongue along his slit to catch the last yummy drop, but her movements became rugged as she bounced atop Cris's cock. He hadn't finished yet and rode her harder. The glistening drop missed her mouth and landed on her breast instead, gracing her pebbled nipple. Already another orgasm was building. She balanced her hands on Cris's thighs and rocked her hips to the sensual tempo he demanded.

"God—Goddamn, honey cake," Cris stammered. "I can feel your cum dripping down my length. You're so tight and so fucking wet. Look at how I glide in and out of you." He swiped a finger along the base of his shaft and tickled the rim of her ass. He raised his hand and stuck his finger in his mouth, tasting her slickness. A raw murmur of delight purred in his chest. "Like fucking strawberry cream. You taste amazing, love. And the way you ride my dick and stroke the length of me . . . I just want to live inside you forever. Fill you with my seed and never let you fucking go . . ."

"Cris . . ."

"Fuck, honey cake. Like a warm cave just for me."

"Cris!" Cyn's voice was harsh this time.

Deaf to his brother's warning tone, Cris's fingers dug deep into Emma's waist, pinning her in place. His hips started to buck. He was about to cum.

"Enough, Cris! Stop!" A sharp slap rang out and ceased Cris's mutterings.

"What? Oh fuck!"

Instantly, Cyn was there. He slid his hands beneath Emma's ass to cradle her weight as he lifted her off his brother.

"Cyn? What are you doing?" She twisted in his arms to look between the brothers.

"Shit," Cris cursed, drawing out the word as he pumped his swollen cock.

Emma gasped in disbelief. She'd thought he was large before . . . How had he possibly fit *that* inside her? A fountain of white erupted into the air, splashing over the back of the couch and coffee table before splattering into Cris's lap. The surge was immense. Gently, Cyn set her down. Was it her imagination or was he shielding her from Cris?

"What in the actual fuck was that?" Cyn yelled.

Cris threw up one of his hands while the other continued to pump his shaft. The sugary scent of buttercream flavored the air. Emma had no doubt he tasted just as delicious as Cyn.

"Don't look at me like that, man. I didn't plan on doing it; it just happened. She felt too fucking good, and I lost my head—"

"She's not yours, Cris. Shit. I said you could only join if you didn't finish inside her. She's mine."

Emma rested her hand on Cyn's forearm. "What's going on?"

Cyn's murderous glare turned to her, then softened. "I'm sorry. I just didn't want him to—"

"But this was your idea. *You* wanted this."

Cyn's lips pressed into a firm line. "I know. And I told him I was okay with everything *but* that. I thought I could trust him."

Emma rounded on Cris. He was still lying on the love seat, spent at last. Euphoria shone in his eyes, yet by the tightness of his jaw, she could tell he was bracing for a reaction. "Did you do that on purpose?"

"Of course not, honey cake. I was going to pull out, but . . ." Cris pointed to his softening cock. Even fully spent, it was still intimidating. "That sweet little cunt was the perfect fit."

Cyn bristled beside her. "I told you, she's not yours."

Emma glanced at Cyn and placed her hands on her hips. "So what? Are you done experimenting? Does it even matter that *I* was enjoying myself? Was this all just some alpha male power play?"

"No, no, Emma. That's not what this is. Please." He brushed his thumb over her wet cheeks. She hadn't even realized she'd started to cry. Cyn shook his head and clasped her hands. "I got lost in my own head. I felt . . . territorial, I guess. You're right. You're not mine. You're allowed to be with whoever you want. Intervening like that was selfish of me, especially when I suggested it in the first place. The magic brought us to life for you. I want *you* to have fun, to explore what *you* like, and if

Cris is the answer, I promise, I won't stand in the way again."

Emma frowned and glanced down at her scarred hands. The once smooth skin was crisscrossed with old burns and calluses. Battle scars as she'd baked cookie after cookie, praying that this time Cyn would come back to her. Could he truly not see her feelings for him? "I want you more. You know that, right? Sorry, Cris." She shot Cris a pointed look, but he didn't appear offended.

Cyn nodded. "I know you tried this for me. And I'm thrilled you were enjoying yourself before I ruined it." He wrapped her in his furnace-like embrace. The scent of spicy cinnamon filled her nostrils when she pressed her cheek against his pec. "Can I make it up to you?"

The divot above Emma's nose wrinkled further. "Maybe."

"Bro, I need at least twenty minutes and a snack," Cris called from the couch.

Cyn ignored him. "Whatever you want, sugar. However you want it, with *whoever* you want, okay?"

"Thank you," Emma said. A small flame of warmth seeped into her frosty tone. "You know, there hasn't been anyone since you."

Cyn's eyes widened a fraction. "What? No one?"

Emma shrugged and wrapped her arms around her exposed breasts. "Jane tried to set me up, but there was no chemistry with any of the other men. I was searching for any resemblance to you, and they all fell short. I *am* yours, Cyn. A little threesome with your gingerbread brother doesn't change that." She smirked. "You should have trusted me."

Cyn hung his head with a chuckle, then pressed a long kiss against her hairline. "You're right." Raising her chin with a gentle touch, he guided her gaze to his. "And I'm sorry I left you alone. But I'm back now, and I swear, as long as you'll have me, I'll be beside you."

A streak of boldness made her ask, "What if I want you forever? Can you promise me that?"

Cyn was silent for a moment. Their earlier conversation swirled through Emma's thoughts. Finally, he said, "We'll figure the magic out, okay? Together."

He couldn't know that for sure, but at least he was open to looking for a way. Emma could live with that for now. Hesitantly, she wrapped her arms around Cyn's tattooed neck and slid her tongue along his lips, easing them open. She hated fighting with him. There was no telling how long they had. She didn't want to waste a second.

Cyn responded ardently and gripped either side of her face to deepen the kiss. He pulled her as close as possible, but it wasn't enough. A carnal ache throbbed in Emma's center. She stretched onto her tiptoes and pressed her breasts against his nude chest. Cyn crouched down to lift her off the floor and hitch her legs above his waist, but when she spread her legs, a bright pain radiated. She tried to downplay her wince, but he was watching too closely.

"Whoa, hang on, sugar. Cris got pretty rough with you. You need a while to heal."

Emma pouted and ran her hand along Cyn's length. "But you might not want me then."

"Sugarcane," Cyn rasped. "I *always* want you."

Emma acquiesced and slowly unwound her legs to slide back down to the floor. Suddenly, a warm hand cupped her ass.

"Sorry for losing control back there," Cris said. He licked his lip. "If you'll let me, I'd love to kiss your pretty pussy until you're all better." He offered a devilish wink and leaned back, slinging his arm over the top of the cushions.

"I . . . um," Emma stammered.

"That's enough, Cris," Cyn ordered. "You need a time-out, too."

"A time-out? What am I, three?"

"You're acting like it."

Cris launched himself off the couch and stood toe to toe with his brother. "You think this is my fault? Look, I was just trying to enjoy myself—"

"By putting her at risk—"

"Boys!" Emma stepped between them and pushed them apart with the heels of her palms. "Stop fighting! Nothing happened, all right?" Both gingerbread men remained silent, staring the other down. "Now, we're all a bit of a mess. Henry had a crude showerhead installed shortly after he bought this bakery. It's nothing grand, but the water's hot and we can all get cleaned up."

"A shower? I've never had one of those," Cris admitted, easing the tension.

"Emma and I shared a bath together. It was nice."

Emma frowned. "I'm afraid the shower won't be as nice as that. I don't have any pretty soaps, but we can at least wash the sweat and other . . . fluids off."

"I'm in." Cris gestured to the cum across his lower abdomen. "I think in this case, there *is* such a thing as too much frosting."

Emma chuckled. He was caked in royal icing, which was hard and cemented onto his dark skin. "I would have to agree with you. Let me blow out these candles and I'll turn it on for you."

"I'll help," Cyn offered. He held out the shirt and skirt Cris had stripped off her body. Now that their passion had cooled, the temperature in the bakery was dropping rapidly. Even the condensation on the windows was starting to clear.

"Thank you." Emma put her arms over her head and smiled as Cyn dressed her like a doll, fitting each piece of clothing into its proper place. She bent down and scooped up the baker's coat. "Your turn."

Cyn slid into the coat's empty sleeves and swiftly did up the buttons. Cris simply slung his coat over his shoulder while he blew out the trio of candles decorating the coffee table.

"What? I'm just going to take it off in a minute anyway." Cris rolled his eyes and swaggered toward the back room. "I'll meet you two lovebirds back here. Just remember, she needs time to heal."

"*I* told *you* that," Cyn tossed over his shoulder.

Cris didn't reply, only threw up his hands and continued on his way. His nude backside sauntered into the shaft of light cast from the kitchen, then disappeared from sight.

"Are you feeling all right?" Cyn asked.

Emma bit her lower lip. "A little sore, but I've had worse."

A dark cloud passed over Cyn's features. He turned her left hand over in his and kissed the scarred flesh. "I still remember finding that burn . . . imagining the pain that monster subjected you to."

Emma stroked Cyn's cheek, compelled to erase the darkness in his eyes. "But thanks to you, he'll never hurt me again."

"It never should have happened in the first place."

"I know, but—"

A loud knock rapped on the glass door, harsh and unexpected. Emma jumped, letting loose a frightened squeal. Cyn's arm drew her closer. The glass was still too foggy to see clearly. Using her sleeve, she wiped the vapor away to reveal a frowning mustache and beady eyes.

"Why is this door locked? It just hit five o'clock. Surely, you're not that punctual a business owner." Nicoli's complaints floated from the other side while he craned his neck to peer inside the dark front room. "Open up. I have news from the judge."

"Who is that?" Cyn asked. His hold didn't relax, and he bristled like a dog sensing a threat.

A pained exhale fell from Emma's lips. "That's Henry's nephew. The one trying to take control of the bakery."

"And he's demanding to come in here? Absolutely not." Cyn moved to block the door, but Emma pushed him out of the way.

"I have to let him in," she whispered. "He spent all afternoon petitioning the judge to reverse Henry's estate. Now that there's a male heir, the bakery will revert to him."

"What does that peacock know about running a bakery? He looks as if he's barely hit puberty."

Emma chuckled and unlocked the door. "Hello, Mr. Dunst."

Nicoli strode across the threshold. A twinge of disgust balanced on the edge of his crinkled nose. "What's going on? Why have you closed so early?"

Emma gestured toward the clock on the wall. "I didn't. It's ten past five. All the other shops closed at 4:30. Tonight was slow. I can't help it if customers don't come in."

"Indeed," Nicoli mumbled. "And who's this? I thought you didn't keep any staff."

She moved to step in front of Cyn. The last thing she needed was this runt examining Cyn too closely. He already seemed suspicious of his uncle's death. "He's not. He's just a friend who stopped by. I needed some help filling orders, and he volunteered."

Nicoli stiffened. "Friend, huh? You don't strike me as a man from this area, sir."

"Quite right," Cyn agreed. "I'm visiting from a different city. I've known Emma for years and was finally able to catch up with her."

Nicoli's gaze traveled up Cyn's imposing form. "Charming. Well, I have private business to discuss with her, so if you don't mind . . ." He waved his hand in the direction of the back room with a challenge in his eyes, daring the big man to argue.

Cyn tensed and glanced at Emma for a silent cue. She offered a subtle nod and crossed her arms, a physical barrier between herself and the haughty relation. Cyn nodded in acknowledgment and walked backward, not breaking eye contact with Nicoli. "I'll be right here if you need anything, Emma."

"Thank you," she replied, a ghost of a smile on her lips. She knew that if she made a single cry, both her gingerbread men would come storming out to defend her.

Nicoli straightened his coat. "Right. I'll get to it. Hells, it's dark in here. And what is that smell? It's like burnt sugar or something. I do hope you're not planning on burning the bakery down now that I'm to inherit it." His mustache twitched with the casual joke, but his eyes were unblinking as he studied her.

Emma waved a flippant hand. "No, nothing like that. I was experimenting with a new recipe and wasn't careful. It got all over my hands and I guess I wasn't paying attention."

A deep frown carved Nicoli's face. "I do hope you take better care of the house than you do the shop.

Honestly, have you fallen so far into spinsterhood after my dear uncle's passing that you don't care how others perceive you?"

A rough bark vibrated low in the back of Emma's throat, but she managed to tamp it down before it escaped from behind her teeth. "Of course, I do. My mind has just been on other things today . . . understandably."

"Quite right. As I stated before, I've been to the records office. As you are currently unmarried, any land holdings and businesses in my uncle's name revert to the closest living male heir. Now that I've returned, the judge has agreed to name me as the proper beneficiary. The paperwork will be drafted tomorrow."

"Tomorrow?" Emma gasped. "So soon?"

"Better to have these matters taken care of sooner rather than later, don't you agree?"

"I . . . I . . . Um . . ."

"There, now. Once everything is settled legally, I'll move my things into the house. Then we'll marry." Nicoli stalked to where Emma stood. "I've always wanted a family. A trio of strapping boys."

"Trio?" Emma's heart sank. It was one thing for Nicoli to force himself into her home but to also force himself into her bed? Her flesh pebbled with goosebumps. This time, she wasn't quick enough to suppress her groan of disgust.

"Does that displease you, Emma?" The way he said her name dripped with misogyny. He had her in his snare, and worse, he knew it. How deplorable was this reality of womanhood? With a single signature, everything she owned and loved was to be ripped away solely based on the fact that she didn't have a sack of wrinkly flesh hanging between her legs.

"As I told you before, I want no part of this, and I don't appreciate the leverage you are so ardently wielding." Her tone was sharp and clipped, leaving no room for misinterpretation. She took two large steps away, angling her body so the coffee table stood between them.

"Unfortunately for you, my sweet, the law favors me and my claim. I will have this charming bakery and you for my wife. There's nothing you can do to stop me, so I suggest you get off your high horse and accept it." Nicoli sneered. "Till tomorrow, dear." With a crisp pivot, he tucked his arms against his sides and exited the shop, ignoring the broken sob that slipped from Emma's lips.

# CHAPTER NINE

It wasn't fair. After Henry's death, Emma built herself up. She'd had to learn the ropes of running a bakery while keeping up with the maintenance demands of the house. She was so proud of what she'd done, and now, with Cyn finally back, it was the perfect way to start her new life. But come morning, she'd be trapped in another marriage, unable to be with the only man she'd fought so hard to find. A handful of tears raced down her cheeks. She locked the door once more and shuffled toward the kitchen.

The shower stall was situated at the far end of the back wall. Nothing sounded better than hitting pause on all her problems and letting the hot water dull her pain and anxiety—anything to delay reality for a few more minutes.

She rounded the corner into the kitchen and shrank back slightly from the bright lights after so long in the dark. Cyn looked up from the steel counter he was cleaning. "Is everything all right?"

Emma tossed her head and pressed her palm to her temple. "No, not really."

"What did he say?" Cris asked.

She dropped her hand. "I don't want to talk about it. Did you guys clean everything?"

"We wanted you to be able to relax. The new cookies are nice and cool too. Sorry again for making it so tense out there. I really wasn't trying to—"

Emma placed her hand on the stammering gingerbread man's chest. Thankfully, he'd slipped into the baker's coat and pants. "It's okay, Cris. Truly. I'm surprised you did all this, though. I really appreciate it."

Cyn's hands wove around Emma's torso and pulled her against his body. It wasn't in a sexual manner but simply meant to comfort. She leaned into his strong arms and inhaled his heady scent. "Of course. We'd do anything for you, especially after seeing the incredible effort you went through trying to bring me back."

Emma shifted her weight to peer up at Cyn. "Because I love . . . loved spending time with you."

His eyebrows arched, but he didn't comment on her slip. Emma's cheeks burned pink, and she tucked her chin. It was far too early to be admitting just how strong her feelings for Cyn had become. She'd had two years to pine for him, but from his perspective, she was a random woman he'd fucked one afternoon. It didn't matter that the sex had been the most incredible high she'd ever known; if Cyn didn't feel the same way, then she'd come off as some crazed clinging nut, obsessed with chaining a fictional cookie to her. No. She had to cork the crazy before she scared him away.

Brushing off Cyn's touch, Emma meandered to the back wall. Boxes were piled high in the basin of the shower well. "Do you mind helping me move these out of here?" Both men jumped at her words. In minutes, they'd moved the clutter out of the way to reveal a tiled alcove with the large rain showerhead perched above. "It's not much, but at least we'll be able to clean up before we head home. That is if you guys are comfortable coming home with me."

"Are you kidding?" Cris laughed. "Don't get me wrong, I love kitchens, but I don't really want to sleep on the floor in front of the oven."

"And I'm not opposed to recreating our previous lovemaking now that we don't have to worry about being disturbed," Cyn added. "Do you want to shower first?"

"Um." Emma assessed the space. It wasn't large by any means, but with the showerhead situated in the center, there was enough room for all of them. "I think we'd all fit. There's not a lot of hot water, and I'd hate to use it all before you guys get a turn."

Cris dropped his pants and tugged the baker's coat over his head, tossing it onto one of the cleared countertops. "Don't need to ask me twice. This looks like it'll be interesting." Now nude, Cris leapt over the short wall that separated the floor from the shower and winked. "Saved a spot for you, love."

Emma wriggled her hips and slid her skirt down

her legs. With a shocked squeak, she realized she'd forgotten to put her panties back on. She pictured them strung across the small bookcase or hanging off one of the plants.

Cris groaned when she bent over to free her ankles from the fabric. "Now, that's a fucking sight." Already, his cock was thickening between his muscular thighs.

Emma peeked at him over her shoulder. "You just saw it out there. Plus, you need to go easy on me, remember?"

"It was too dark out there to fully appreciate you, honey cake. Seeing your sweet pussy all aglow?" Cris inhaled sharply and tossed his head. "It'll be a fucking challenge not to ravage you."

"Are you not up for it?" Emma kicked her skirt across the floor and ran her hands down the swell of her ass.

"Fuck. Guess I'll find some way to control myself."

"If you don't, I'll lay your ass out. You got me, little brother?" Cyn's commanding tone thundered, reverberating off the steel appliances.

Cris rolled his eyes and swatted at his erection. "No penetration. Unless she asks for it."

"You're awfully cocky, aren't you?" Emma smirked. Her fingers curled around the hem of her shirt, then lifted the fabric over her head. Her breasts swayed with the motion, her dark nipples flirting for attention.

Cris gestured again to his lower half. "That's all your fault, sweetheart. You're the one who molded me this monster. I'm simply putting it to good use."

"Enough, Cris," Cyn ordered. "Let her relax a little. Don't you need any time before you rebound?"

"This is my first time alive, *and* I get to play with her perfect body? I don't know how you're *not* ready to go."

Cyn shrugged. "I can't argue with that. Emma is perfection." He purred and spanked her lightly on the ass.

"Easy, man!" Cris reprimanded.

Emma threw up her hands. "Honestly, I feel like I'm back in junior high. Let's just take a shower and see where we're all at after." She tried to sound authoritative but the idea of another threesome on the couch made her sex pulse with desire. Of the three of them, someone had to remain in control. If she let them in on her naughty fantasy, they'd never get anything done. Besides, she *was* sore from Cris earlier. The warm water would feel amazing and soothe both her physical and emotional points of pain.

With a toss of her long hair, Emma threw the kinky visuals from her mind and joined Cris. Her teeth chattered, exposed as she was on the cold tile. There wasn't a door or even a curtain to shield them. Henry had installed the shower for practicality rather than luxury. Thinking back, she could only recall him using it once or twice.

"Cyn? Can you check those boxes before joining us? I think I remember seeing little soap bars and some towels in one of them."

"Sure, but don't stand there shivering on my account. Turn on the water and get—"

"Thanks, brother," Cris said before Cyn finished speaking. "I'm guessing this chain turns it on?" He stretched and clicked the chain. The latch released, and ice-cold water spilled out. Frigid droplets splashed Emma's bare skin, and she shrieked.

"Damn! That's cold. I thought you said it would be hot?"

"I-I did. It h-has to warm up a b-bit first," Emma said. "Sorry. I w-wasn't thinking."

"It's all right. I remember waiting in the icebox while my dough chilled. In the meantime, I'm sure I can come up with a way to warm you."

"Cris," Cyn warned, his hand buried up to his elbow in the first box.

"Do you want her to freeze?"

For a minute, Cyn didn't respond. Then his shoulders sagged. "Just . . . go slow."

"And you won't stop me this time?"

Cyn shook his head. "No. I made a promise."

Emma could barely hear Cyn's words over her chattering teeth and the hiss and spit of the falling water. Cyn smiled encouragingly, then continued to pore over the box's contents. A few seconds later, he came up empty and moved to another.

Cold mist enveloped Emma. She stood as far out of the spray as possible, arms pulled tight to preserve what little body heat she had left while her toes curled and her knees knocked together.

"There, there. I've got you." Cris's baritone whispered in her ear. His palms clasped her upper arms and rubbed their length, trying to use the friction to warm her. The prickling mist vanished when he stepped in front of her, his back acting as a shield.

"Aren't you c-cold?"

"Nah. I've got a lot more meat on my bones than you. Is this helping?"

"Yes. Thank y-you."

"Nothing worse than being cold. I don't know how Frosty does it. Give me a warm fire over an icy dark night any day."

"F-Frosty? Like the snowman?"

"That's him. He's into some *weird* stuff."

Slowly, feeling seeped back into Emma's toes. "Like what?"

Cris chuckled. "I'll put it this way. He makes what we did out there seem tame. Plus he's into electro-play."

Emma's eyes bulged. "You're making that up."

"Maybe I am." Cris grinned devilishly. Without pausing his hands, he leaned forward and captured her trembling lips. Heat radiated off his body and Emma melted into him. His mouth yielded heat while his tongue playfully danced with hers.

His hands slowed, meandering to her lower back, then pulled her tight against him. Emma almost moaned; he was so warm. Her arms relaxed her armor-like pose and snaked around Cris's torso, resting on his well-defined hips. She couldn't remember carving the cookie with abs, but Cris's physique was obvious beneath her touch.

Skillfully, Cris deepened their kiss, taking it from playful to passionate. His full lips moved sensually atop hers, and his tongue's strokes grew languid, lulling her into a passionate embrace. Emma's shivers calmed as his heat encompassed her. Desire boiled within and her pussy clenched with need. It didn't matter that she was sore. All that mattered was that she wanted him, needed him to fill her again and satisfy the throbbing ache. Her cunny pulsed against him, and his erection speared her belly.

"Cris," Emma breathed over his lips.

"Hold that thought, love. I promised to go slow and be gentle, and I'm a gingerbread man of my word."

Faster than Emma could comprehend the movement, Cris maneuvered her under the stream of water. She gasped, flinching against the imminent blast of cold water, but hot, almost scorching droplets drizzled onto her shoulders instead, making her skin tingle with heat.

Emma sighed. "So much better." Tipping her head back, she let the water run its fiery fingers through her hair and massage her scalp. It felt so good as if she were thawing out. She was so focused on the water, she missed when Cris's lips trailed to her ear, down her neck. His tongue flicked, branding her skin while he delighted in her flesh. It was so new, this feeling of being devoured, like he couldn't get enough of her body.

Emma's hips rolled, searching for Cris's cock. She slipped her hand from around his waist and dropped it to his shaft. He was thick and hard, just as eager as she was. His large hand reached up and circled Emma's neck like a choker. He squeezed and stole her next breath.

"Do you know how hot you look with the water cascading down your curves? A beautiful siren made just for me." Emma tugged on his cock, desperate to align it with her center. "Do you want this dick?"

"Yes," Emma whispered.

"You want this big dick buried in that tight cunny?"

"Yes."

Cris squeezed her neck harder and edged the crown closer to her slit. "Sing for me. Tell me how much you want this thick cock pounding into that pussy."

"Please, Cris." Emma groaned around the hand necklace. "Please, I want you to fuck me."

"Hmm, good, but you can do better."

She pumped her hand up and down his shaft, not relinquishing her hold. "Fuck me, Cris. I need you to fuck me, right fucking now," Emma whined. Between the heat and the pressure on her windpipe, she was beginning to see stars.

"But I thought you were too sore from the pounding I gave you earlier. Do you really think you're ready to ride this big dick again?"

Emma increased her hold and lifted her right leg, opening herself up to him. Hot water ran down her center, burning the sensitive skin but she didn't care. All she could think about was Cris and his mammoth cock only an inch away. She guided the tip of him forward and rubbed her slickness over him.

"What do you think? You've got me so fucking wet."

Desire ignited in Cris's dark eyes, but he hesitated. "I don't want to hurt you."

"Just put it in already. If I can't take it, I'll tell you. I'm a big girl."

Lust flared, and his pupils blew wide, eyes dark as the obsidian coal used to light the ovens. Water flowed down his brow and pooled on his lashes. Fuck, he was so sexy.

"You are. You're a naughty girl who needs this dick, aren't you?"

"Yes. Give it to me, Cris. Fill my cunt with that cock. Make me scream. Make me—fuck!"

Cris thrust into her, driving his shaft deep into her center. Emma balked at his girth and swore when he withdrew completely only to slam back into her. His arms swooped under her legs and pinned her in place against the wall. She wound her arms around his neck, clinging on.

"Fuck, fuck, fuck, Cris!" His rhythm was insane. Already her orgasm drummed, cresting toward release.

"Your fault, love. You're so fucking wet. Watch the way I slide in and out of this sweet cunt. Look at how you weep for me."

"Keep going. Harder. Give me more, Cris."

"More? You hear that, Cyn? She's begging for more." Cris paused his thrusts and withdrew to the tip, teasing her with the slightest pressure.

"Loud and clear," Cyn answered. He dropped the stack of towels he carried onto the edge of a nearby counter and bounced a rectangular box in his palm. "I'm not sure she's ready, though."

Cris snickered. "Me neither. Both of us would be too much for her."

Emma sighed and tried to pull Cris closer, to drive his cock in deeper, but the way he held her restricted her movement. "I've already taken both of you at once. Hurry up! The hot water won't last much longer."

Cyn stepped into the steam, eyes burning with lust. "Not like this, sugar." His voice was so gravelly, she could feel it in her chest.

Emma frowned. "What do you mean?"

"You already know the pleasure we can give your sweet pussy, but there's more, love. So much more," Cris whispered.

She started to reply but Cris's thumb slipped down and tapped her ass, circling the puckered ridge. Emma's eyes bulged. "You mean—"

"Absolutely."

"Only if you want to, Emma," Cyn added. "And if we try and it's too much, just say so and we'll stop immediately. Right, Cris?"

"Yeah. I only care about giving you pleasure, honey cake." As if to prove his point, Cris grabbed his shaft and slid it farther in, pounding into her with four quick bursts.

"Fuck, Cris. That's not fair. You know what you're doing." Emma bit her lip and sank lower onto his cock. He felt so good filling her, but never before had she explored anal play. Would it feel good? Cyn would never do anything to hurt her, and part of her *was* curious. The idea of both guys filling her at once created an intoxicating visual. "You'll stop if I don't like it?"

"Yes," both men answered simultaneously.

"And you'll be gentle?"

"Always, sugar."

"Besides, you're so wet, it won't hurt at all. I could always work my tongue in there first to make you comfortable." Cris grinned and slammed his cock into her a few more times. In his last thrust, he left his dick in as deep as he could. "Crumbs, being buried in this pussy is like kryptonite. I can't wait to feel how tight that ass is, delight in the way it hugs me."

"You?" Emma gasped. "You're the one going to take me there? But . . . you're so thick."

"Would you rather I did, sugar?" Cyn asked.

Emma nodded, color flooding her cheeks. "Yes, and I—" She pinched her lips shut, but Cris read her thoughts easily.

"You trust him more than me?" A dark chuckle resounded as Cris moved. He dropped her from where she was perched against the wall and drew a startled moan from her lips when his cock shifted and hit her G-spot. "You should. I already lost control once. Who knows what would happen back there?"

Emma knew he was teasing, but his words made her shiver and her pussy clench. He spoke like he was only interested in using her, but she had to admit, she didn't hate it. Cyn's warm hands ran along her curves when he joined them in the falling water.

"Don't worry, sugarcane. I know what you like."

Emma sighed, nerves aflutter. "Okay. Let's give it a try, then."

"Fuck, that's my girl." Cris gave her a wide smile. "But if we're going to do this, I need my dick back for a bit. There's no way I can stay buried in that treasure chest without climaxing while my brother starts to play." With a swift kiss, he pulled out and gently turned her body. His cock glistened with her wetness, straining for her warmth, but he was in control. For now.

"What do we do now? How do we start?" Emma asked, wide-eyed.

Cyn moved and kneeled behind her. His hands gripped her waist, and he gave her cheek a quick bite. "Just stand there, sugar. I need to make sure you're primed for me so it doesn't hurt."

Emma swallowed her trepidation. "Okay."

Without another word, Cyn's tongue lapped at her opening, warm and wet. The sensation was foreign but sent waves of pleasure through her frame. It was so erotic, so forbidden. Just when she thought these boys couldn't do anything else to rock her world ... He delved deeper and slipped his tongue inside, offering her sensual kisses as if he were praying to an idol. Emma's nipples hardened beneath the hot current while he tasted and teased, giving tiny love bites. She inhaled and stuttered when he pressed his tongue fully against her and fluttered wildly.

"Told you you'd like it," Cris said. "Now, it's my turn. Can't let this perfect cunny feel left out." Taking hold of his cock, he tapped it against her clit, rubbing her swollen pearl with the crown.

Emma moaned as the competing pleasure consumed her. What was it going to feel like with both their cocks pounding into her? She closed her eyes, and when she opened them, Cris was pulling his fingers out of his mouth. A moment later, he plunged two fingers inside her while the pad of his thumb circled her clit. Punctuating sighs filled the air as she adjusted to their tempos. Slick coated her thighs; her body couldn't help but respond. The orgasm Cris had been coaxing out of her ignited. She ached to be filled again.

Another finger slid along her taint and entered her ass up to the first knuckle. Emma moaned, loving the tightness. She rolled her hips to take him deeper.

"You okay with this, sugar?"

Emma nodded, eyes rolling into the back of her head when Cris swirled her clit faster.

"I need you to verbalize your consent before I continue," Cyn demanded.

"Fuck, it feels good. Keep going."

"Good girl. I think she's ready, Cris. I can taste her arousal."

"Excellent, because my dick is throbbing."

Cyn rose to his feet and turned Emma's body so she was sandwiched between them. "You go first, then I'll enter her."

"You got it."

The pipe gurgled, and the water temperature cooled just a fraction, but it was enough to register on Emma's skin. "Hurry, boys. The water is starting to cool."

"Come here then, love, and ride this dick," Cris ordered.

Before Emma could obey, he scooped her off her feet and hiked her legs around his waist, his warm cock already nudging her slick entrance. She arched back, desperate to take him, and with a sly grin, Cris thrust into her. A guttural groan rumbled in the back of her throat as he held her ass and pounded into her in rapid succession. Her breasts bounced, inviting him to lean forward and suck on a peaked nipple.

"Fuck, Cris, yes! Right there!" Another spear of heat caressed the back of her thigh. She'd nearly forgotten about Cyn . . . and his intentions.

"Still ready for me, sugarcane?"

Emma pushed the small pit of fear to the depths of her mind and nodded. She ached with need, ached to be ravaged, to be fucked into oblivion.

"Let me know if you need me to stop," Cyn said quietly, but his tone was firm.

"Okay."

Cris ceased his thrusts for a minute while Cyn lined the tip of his cock up with her ass. A sharp thrill zinged through her when his heat grazed her there, followed by intense pressure. Emma held her breath. Would he even be able to enter? Her worries were erased a second later when Cyn slid the tip into her ass with ease thanks to his expert tongue.

Emma inhaled at a pinch of pain but it vanished once Cyn started to move. Slowly, he thrust, causing her to ride up and down. It didn't hurt. In fact, it felt incredible to be so full. Her entire body reeled from the stimulation.

"Oh my God," Emma cried. Cris resumed, matching his brother's pace. Cyn's broad hands palmed her ass and forced her cheeks ever wider as he sank his cock halfway in.

"Fucking crumbs, you're so tight, sugar. The way your ass is milking my dick is insane." Emma moaned in response, prompting Cyn to pump faster, sliding her along his length. "Fuck, I didn't think it'd feel this good."

"Yes! Give it to me, boys. Holy fuck, I can barely take it."

"Should we stop?"

"No, no! Don't you dare stop!"

Encouraged, both deepened their thrusts and relinquished control, giving into their carnal desire. Groans, moans, and sighs filled the air as a collection of lips, teeth, and hands trailed, squeezed, and slapped at her body. Emma was lost to a writhing sea of sensation, unaware of where one body ended and the other began. It was beyond kinky, pure savage lovemaking as both men explored her body and took their own pleasures. She loved the way they filled her, pushing her to the brink of delirious destruction.

Cris's hand fit around her neck and pulled her lips to his. His tongue ran along her teeth, and soon they were both drowning in the kiss. Cyn's hold on her ass squeezed as he pushed even deeper, and his groan of ecstasy stirred a fluttering in her chest.

"I can't last much longer, sugarcane."

"I'm close, too," Cris agreed against Emma's lips. "What about you, love? Are you ready to cum all over this dick?" He released the pressure on her windpipe and slid his hand up to grip her jaw. "Answer me, Emma. Are you ready to cum?"

"Yes!" Emma growled and threw her head back at the same moment Cris used his other thumb to stimulate her clit once more.

Cris recaptured her mouth, bruising her under his kiss, and gave her swollen lip a quick nip. His hand traveled to her breasts and slapped at her nipple twice. "Then show me. Milk these cocks, sweetheart, and take our cum like a good little slut."

Emma rolled her hips slowly, savoring every wonderful inch of them.

"Fuckkkk, sugar. I love this little hole. I can't—" Cyn exhaled and dropped his head as he came, fingers digging into her flesh.

"That's it, honey cake. Take us. Take everything we give you," Cris said just as his cock triggered her own orgasm to implode.

Emma surrendered to the swell of pleasure and rode her climax in the most powerful wave of ecstasy. Cris swore a second later and released his load as well, pounding deep inside her one last time. Emma's eyes fluttered toward the ceiling while ribbons of pleasure rocketed through her. Both gingerbread men strained to keep their dicks buried in her until she was fully satisfied. A final wave claimed her, and her pussy pulsed, forcing Cris's cock out. Cyn withdrew his right after, and together they exhaled a satiated breath. Warmth trickled down the insides of Emma's thighs. Thick white frosting-like cum dripped onto the tile floor.

"Damn, that's sexy watching my seed pour out of you," Cris whispered roughly.

Cyn ran his nose along Emma's jaw and kissed her. "You were amazing, sugar. Thank you for trying something new." He stepped away and came back, holding two identical white bars.

"What's this?" Emma asked, shivering slightly. The water was now lukewarm at best.

"Soap. Let's get you cleaned up. Sorry we used all the hot water."

"Worth it," Emma answered, peeking up at him through her lashes. Embarrassment arrested her. She was shy at the simple thought of washing herself in their presence. Somehow, it seemed far more intimate than sinking onto their cocks.

Cyn tossed one of the bars to Cris, then held the other one under the stream until it was thoroughly drenched. Emma could relate. He rubbed it between his palms until a frothy lather bloomed, then passed it to her.

"Don't you want to use it first?" Emma asked.

Cyn shook his head. "You first, sugar. As much as I enjoyed painting you with my frosting, you deserve to feel fresh and clean."

Emma shifted her weight and accepted the soap. From the slight movement, she could feel how the viscous liquid coated her skin. "You've got a point." She laughed. "Thanks." She leaned forward and kissed him, inhaling his intoxicating aroma. Not even the shower or the crisp scent of the soap could mask his cinnamon scent.

Twirling into the cooling waterfall, Emma hurriedly covered her body in bubbles. Next to her, Cris mirrored her, concentrating on his lower extremity until his cock was nearly covered.

"This stuff is fun. It tingles when the suds pop," he said, clearly enjoying his first shower.

"Guess we'll have to utilize this a bit more, then," Emma teased.

Cris slid his arm around her waist while she tipped her head back to wash her long hair. "Only if you join me."

Cyn swatted Cris's forearm. "Back off and give her some space."

"Geez, buzzkill much?"

Cyn leveled Cris with a hard stare. "Stop thinking about your dick and consider someone else for a change."

Cris saluted Cyn, then finished rubbing the bar of soap over the rest of his body. "Yes, sir, captain, sir."

Emma laughed, but Cyn's frown deepened. "So glad you could join us this time, brother."

"Me too. Your sex would have been super vanilla without me."

Emma splashed water at Cris. "For your information, we did just fine without you before."

"Oh, just fine, huh? Sounds hot."

She smacked his shoulder and tossed Cyn her bar of soap.

"Okay, okay, truce," Cris conceded. "Maybe I'm just jealous I wasn't there."

Emma collected her hair and dragged it over her shoulder to squeeze out the excess water. "Aw. Well, you're here now."

"Thank the ovens." Cris arched his eyebrows and shot her a wicked grin that promised more.

"Cyn's right, though. Give it a rest. I'm cold and hungry. No more sex until this baker is fed."

"I'll give you something to eat—"

"Cris!" both Cyn and Emma yelled.

"Fine, fine." Cris put up his hands in surrender and stood beneath the falling water. "Food first. Though technically, I *was* food so . . ."

Emma leaned over the short wall and grabbed one of the towels Cyn had dug up from the boxes. The fluffy terry cloth felt glorious on her damp skin when she settled into its plush embrace. "Not the kind of food I'm hungry for at the moment."

A wounded Cris clutched a soapy hand to his chest. "We'll see, honey cake."

Emma smirked and wrapped the towel tighter around her body, not correcting its positioning when the curve of her ass peeked out from beneath its cover. She heard a groan behind her, followed by inaudible mumbling, but neither of them could satisfy her current hunger.

# CHAPTER TEN

Half an hour later, the trio leaned against the front counter, savoring warm buttered toast, apple pie, and leftover chocolate chip croissants. Emma's hair dried in mermaid-like ringlets, wavy and golden around her shoulders. One of the boxes in the back contained a pile of Henry's old clothes. The too-small material was comical on the two gingerbread men, but at least they were clothed in something besides soiled baker's coats. It also helped that their ardent cocks were properly caged for a bit too. Now she could focus on more pressing matters, like how in the hell she was going to evade Nicoli and the judge's order come tomorrow morning.

She clapped her hands to rid her fingertips of clinging breadcrumbs and stuck her thumb in her mouth to suck away the melted chocolate. Maybe she could go to court and plead her case? After all, she'd profitably run the bakery for two years and tended to her home independently. What about her current predicament suggested she couldn't take care of herself or required a man to rescue her? Her forlorn sigh puffed into the air as she rubbed her temples. There had to be a solution.

"What did that man say to you?" Cyn asked after he swallowed the last bite of his pastry.

Emma frowned. "The judge agreed to name Nicoli as Henry's official heir. Unless I can exploit some legal loophole by 9:00 a.m., he gets everything. Including me."

"That's it?" Cris asked.

"That's it. I have nothing to fight back with."

"But that's wrong." Cyn pushed himself off the glass display. "You're not some family heirloom to be inherited or passed down. You're a human being. Why shouldn't you be able to remain independent?"

Emma wiped her palms on the front of her skirt and shrugged. "Not according to the antiquated laws. This is rural Pennsylvania. Women's rights aren't exactly at the top of the ballots out here."

"Wait, let me get this straight," Cris said. "If you were married, you'd be able to keep ownership of the bakery as long as your new husband gave you permission?"

"Pretty much because it'd be in his name, too."

"So then, why don't you get married?"

Emma threw up her hands. "That's what Nicoli is proposing. He wants to step into Henry's shoes."

Cris shook his head. "No, not to him. Marry Cyn. That way, you retain ownership and your home, and this guy has no leg to stand on because you've rightly inherited your late husband's estate."

Silence swelled in the dimly lit shop as Emma's eyes widened with hope and possibility. She ran her tongue along her lower lip. Would that save her from Nicoli and his greed? Her excitement soured in the next moment when she turned and glanced at Cyn. Rather than sharing in her joy, his expression was tight, jaw steeled and brow furrowed. Anxiety dropped in her chest like an anchor, manifesting in the habitual wringing of her hands, as if a certain number of revolutions would alter his countenance.

"What's wrong, brother?" Cris wondered.

So she hadn't imagined his disapproval.

Cyn ran his hand along his scalp and grimaced. "Nothing, it's just . . . I'm not sure that's a good idea."

The bundle of writhing nerves in Emma's chest constricted. "You don't want to marry me?" She hated the way her voice squeaked, high and pathetic. "But earlier you said you wanted to be with me."

Cyn exhaled a defeated sigh, dropped his hand, and reached for her. "I do. Of course, I want to be with you, but—" He stopped speaking and looked at Cris. "Can you give us some space for this?"

Cris hesitated, looking to Emma for direction. His usual joking manner was gone, replaced with genuine concern. Concern for *her*. Did she really look that miserable? The only man she'd ever developed feelings for had just admitted to having reservations about marrying her, but she hadn't dissolved into tears. Yet. Given everything, she was composing herself remarkably well.

"Are you okay if I leave?" Cris asked.

"I'm not going to hurt her," Cyn seethed.

"Seems like you're already doing a pretty good job of that." Cris's features darkened.

Emma offered him a weak smile and crossed her arms over her chest. "I'll be fine."

"All right. I'll be in the kitchen *when* you change your mind." Cris turned and shot his brother a disappointed look as he passed.

Cyn released another sigh once they were alone and stepped toward her, his arms open and inviting—a direct opposition to his cutting refusal. "Please let me explain. I can see your mind whirring with every negative thought possible, but believe me when I say my worries have *nothing* to do with you." He stopped a few inches away, letting her decide if she wanted to accept his embrace.

Clearing her throat, Emma blinked back tears and maintained her position. "Then what is it? What is it about us that you don't want to make permanent?"

"But that's just it," Cyn said, dropping his arms to his sides. "I'm not permanent. What will happen if we do get married and I die? Turn back into a cookie and crumble to dust? I can't leave you vulnerable like that again. And what will happen when Nicoli sees you've been widowed a second time? Will they accept another death associated with you so easily? Especially mine, one where you can't even produce a real body? I can't bear to think of the repercussions you'd face for something beyond your control. If I die, Nicoli will swoop in faster than it'd take to sweep my crumbs off the floor."

Emma wanted to disagree, but it wasn't hard to imagine the bleak future Cyn described. She could see Nicoli with a wicked smirk on his face while they arrested her, or worse, threw her into an asylum when she tried to explain where her second husband had gone.

"I have no idea how long the magic that brought me to life will last. Does that make sense? I only want what's best for you."

Emma nodded and took a step closer in silent forgiveness. She understood and appreciated that his refusal came from a place of love, but the rejection and the probability of a future without Cyn stung beyond description. "I know," she whispered. "I wish there were a way to make you truly real. Have you ever heard of a way to make the magic permanent?"

A crooked frown dominated Cyn's features. "Truthfully, I never should have existed in the first place. I don't know anything regarding the magic, let alone how to influence it." His words were soft but void of hope as if he'd already given up.

"Then what do I do? Nicoli won't leave me alone unless I marry someone else first. How is tying myself to a random stranger any better than being his wife? I want you and only you. And I want to be with you whenever and however I want. Whether that's walking down the street holding hands or letting you bend me over the counter in broad daylight. All I want is you. Anyone else would provide an empty existence." Fat tears raced down her face, salting her lips.

Cyn tried to staunch her tears with his sleeve. "I feel the same way. If there was anything I could do to stay with you forever, you know I would, right?"

Emma nodded and sniffled. She pressed her face into Cyn's warm shoulder. His cinnamon scent enveloped her, but instead of its usual comfort, panic overwhelmed her. How much longer did they have? How much longer until she was left with nothing but crumbs and his fading scent? He held her for several minutes, neither of them feeling the need to speak. It just felt good to be together, even if they couldn't quantify exactly how long that would be.

"Maybe I can find a way to dispose of Nicoli? I'm sure I could deliver a fatal dose of some herb or plant into his food or drink. Then we could be together." Emma said it jokingly, but there was an undercurrent of truth to her words.

"No, sugar. For one so pure and gentle, you've already seen far too much death. I don't want that for you." Cyn kissed the top of her head and rubbed her back. He was trying to comfort her, but the reality of their impossible situation struck her heart like one of Cupid's arrows, only this one was designed to fester rather than bloom.

# CHAPTER ELEVEN

The knitted scarf kissed Emma's neck. "Are you sure you don't want to come with us?" She burrowed her chin into the worn fabric as if she could already feel the biting wind. "The couch isn't that comfortable."

Cris waved his hand. "I'll be fine. From what I recall, it was plenty comfortable. I need to clean it up anyway before your customers arrive tomorrow."

Emma chewed on her bottom lip. "I don't like the idea of you staying by yourself."

"Not to worry, love. I'm a big boy. Plus, I'll feel better keeping watch in case that sleazy guy tries to sneak in before you get back."

"That's not a bad idea," Cyn said.

"Genius does strike from time to time." Cris settled back onto the one clean cushion and relaxed, threading his hands behind his head.

Emma's trepidation transformed into a smile. She had to admit, it *was* a good idea. "I guess that way I won't be blindsided if he strikes early . . ."

Cris shrugged. The movement made his biceps bulge.

"Great. It's settled, then. I'll keep an eye on everything here and the two of you can enjoy some *alone* time."

Emma snorted. "I really don't think Cyn is interested in doing it again."

A large hand palmed the curve of her ass. "I'm always ready to go when it comes to you, sugar," Cyn whispered in a husky tone.

Emma shoved him away. "Fine, I recant my statement, but let the record show that *I'm* exhausted. Let's go, Romeo."

Cyn's hand slid north to rest on her lower back instead. "I like it when you're bossy."

Emma gave him another knock with her hip, but his muscular frame barely budged. "All right. We'll see you in the morning, Cris. Help yourself to anything you want except for my orders. Those are labeled! Good night."

Cris offered a half-hearted wave and pushed himself off the couch, heading toward the small sink. "Night, guys."

Cyn settled a knit hat atop Emma's crown, then held the door open for her. "Night, brother. Behave."

"Give me some credit," Cris called after them as the door closed.

"He'll be fine, Cyn." Emma pulled the collar of her coat up to shield her neck from winter's frigid bite. "He's a grown man—well, a grown cookie, I guess." Falling in step with Cyn, she nestled into the crook of his arm, delighting in the heat that radiated off him even in the cold.

"I know. I'm just ribbing him. It's what brothers do."

"I wish I knew. I was never close with any of my siblings. We were always working. There was no time for games or make-believe and no secrets at night because we were all bone-tired."

Casually, they strolled through the sleepy town. Light snowflakes twirled in the air, kissing her lashes and pink cheeks. All the other businesses were closed, save for the small diner serving hot plates of turkey and mashed potatoes. Lampposts burned. Their orange flames danced above their heads to guide them home.

"That sounds sad," Cyn said softly.

Emma shrugged. The only sound for the next block was their feet crunching atop the thin layer of freshly fallen snow.

"You're the oldest, right?" Cyn asked.

"Yup. My sister is three years younger than me."

"Have you ever thought of going back home? Especially after your husband died?"

"Not really. After my mother passed, my dad . . . Well, let's just say we don't get along. My marriage to Henry really deepened the resentment I used to try so hard to ignore. Maybe in a few more years, I'll go back. My sister might have a family of her own by then."

"Family, like kids?"

Emma smiled. "Yeah. My sister always talked about having a large family when we were younger. I think she was more interested in her children doing all the chores rather than quenching any maternal need, but still."

"What about you? Do you want children?"

The snow fell faster. The once-mini flakes grew to fluffy wisps across the sky.

"I'm not sure. While baking with my mother, I would envision doing the same with my own child one day, but then I married Henry, and I refused to bring a baby into the world to be subjected to his cruelty. Now that he's gone, I haven't even considered what comes next. I've been so busy with the shop and trying to craft the perfect recipe to bring you back. There hasn't been much time to think of much else."

Cyn paused and spun her to face him. Cupping her face in his hands, he gazed into her amber eyes. "I'm so sorry."

"It's fine—"

"No. I never should have left you, but I feel even more guilt for the way my recreation dominated your life afterward. I left you with no energy to put yourself first. That's not okay, Emma."

"No, I mean, I wanted to . . ." She tried to explain, but the reality of his words hit hard. From the moment he crumbled to cookie bits in front of her, she'd thought of nothing else. Not her family, nor her goals, nor what she wanted from life. She'd become obsessed, consumed with baking him again. The bakery and all its success had been nothing more than a happy accident. She *was* proud of herself. Yet even then, failure ate away at her accomplishments. She'd been unable to recreate the magic that gave her Cyn all those months ago, and she couldn't stop herself from fixating on that.

Even now, with him standing in front of her, she was gripped with anxiety. If she lost him a second time, what would that do to her mental state? She'd have to start all over. Chasing a fantasy while the real world and her real life passed her by. What if it took her ten years next time? Cyn would return in his gorgeous glory, but she'd be pushing middle age—silver streaks in her blonde hair and crow's feet around her eyes with nothing to show for all the time gone by. She was doomed either way.

She'd gone on dates at Jane's urging, but not one man captivated her like Cyn. He'd ruined her in the best way, but it was a curse too. For if she couldn't be with him, she refused to be with anyone. No one else would ever measure up.

"You deserve so much more in this life, Emma," Cyn whispered. "So much more than what I can give you."

Emma threaded her fingers through his. "But you're all I want."

A long sigh slipped between them as Cyn's gaze lowered. "But don't you want children of your own to laugh and snuggle with? To watch them learn and grow? Even if I manage to stay this time, I can't give you that. I can't have children." The heartache in his voice was tangible.

"Then I'll bake us some. They'd be your adorable mini-mes."

A sad smile pulled at the corners of his lips. "Maybe, but they wouldn't be real. They would never grow or mature. They'd be another falsehood in this strange dream."

Tears pooled in Emma's eyes. "But it's such a great dream."

"I know, sugar, but I don't want to hurt you again."

Emma tilted her head and reared back. "What are you saying? You don't want to be with me at all because no matter what, I'll get hurt?" She worked to keep her voice even, but the way her chest constricted forced her question up several octaves.

"No. That's not it at all. All I'm trying to do is prepare you for when I—"

"When you leave me again," Emma finished. "Is this going to be a biannual thing, then? You return for a solid night of fucking and then dissolve into a cookie?"

"You're upset—"

"Why shouldn't I be? You show up after two years, fuck me until your heart's content, and now you're ready to move on because you're bored."

"Emma, please. That's not what I'm saying."

Tears blinded her and rage deafened any explanation Cyn tried to cook up. "The thing is you won't even try. You won't even give us a shot because you're so terrified it won't work and you'll hurt me, but what do you call this?" Emma pointed to the tears racing down her face. "You think it's easier to be abandoned on purpose than by accident, is that it? At least before, you wanted to stay with me."

Cyn tried to embrace her once more, but she pushed him off. "You're right. I'm sorry. I thought having this discussion would make it easier when the magic ran out, but I was wrong. It's your life, Emma. I have no right to tell you how you should live it. I want nothing more than to be with you, for every second going forward, for as long as you'll have me. I want to cook you breakfast, listen while you sing, and hold you through the night. I'm yours, Emma."

His words cocooned around her breaking heart, soothing the cracks like a balm until the surface was smooth and unmarred. Emma collapsed against his chest, seeking the haven of his heartbeat. There, under his flesh, was a steady beat that matched her own. That was all the proof she needed. He was real enough. All she was asking for was a chance to see if their attraction could bloom into something deeper. She met his obsidian gaze.

"Thank you. You have no idea how much that means to me." Emma leaned in and pressed her lips to his.

"But I do," Cyn replied. "Because you're all I want, too." His arms braceleted her again, but this time, she didn't push him away and instead nuzzled into his chest. "Come on. I need to get you home."

The kitchen greeted them after Emma unwound her scarf and draped their coats over the olive wingback chair. Rushing water hissed as she filled a glass and leaned over the low front apron sink. The liquid was cool as it slid down her throat. Had she had anything to drink since Cyn's resurgence? Whenever she was with him, everything else was trivial, but her body had no objection to voicing its need for sleep now. Her eyelids had suddenly taken on the characteristic of lead weights. She could hardly keep them open.

Setting the glass on the counter, Emma turned and assessed Cyn. He was leaning against the doorframe to the hallway with a queer look on his face. "What is it?"

"This is where we met, remember?" His voice was honey while his eyes swept the tidy kitchen.

Emma chuckled. "Of course. I expected to find a cookie, but instead, I found an empty tray—and you."

"Surprise."

"That's an understatement." Emma crossed the small room and stopped in front of him. "Maybe even more so because you were stark naked."

"As were you, I recall," Cyn teased.

Gently, they began to sway back and forth, their footsteps carrying them to the bedroom.

Emma leaned over and blew out the candle, plunging the cozy space into darkness. "I'd just gotten out of the bath and thought I was alone. Besides, being naked is more fun."

"You're right about that." Cyn kissed her and hoisted her onto his hips, giving her ass a firm squeeze. "What do you say we reenact that? I think we've been clothed long enough."

"It's barely been an hour!" Emma squealed when Cyn fisted the hem of her blouse and yanked it over her head. "Ah! You're incorrigible." Her breasts bounced over the bra's cups while her hips rolled of their own accord against his toned stomach.

After slipping out of his borrowed shirt with ease, Cyn let the rumpled material fall to the floor. His lips trailed down the curve of Emma's neck to the sensitive skin along her collarbone. A warm wet sensation glided over the swell of her tits when he dipped his head farther.

"Cyn," Emma moaned. She knew she should sleep. She needed to be at her best tomorrow to face Nicoli, but she couldn't keep her body from responding to him. Her hips rocked, her sex aching to be touched.

Cyn hummed low in his throat. The next thing she knew, soft blankets cradled her back when he set her down atop the quilt.

"I want you to know I got a new bed," Emma whispered as she ran her hands along the stark ridges of Cyn's biceps.

He lifted his head from where his mouth was buried between her breasts and quirked an eyebrow. "Oh really?"

Emma nodded. The only light came from the three-quarter moon peeking through the window. "I remember how much it bothered you, so after everything, I used the bakery's first month's profit to buy a brand-new one. It hasn't been broken in yet."

Cyn released the clasp on her bra, spilling her breasts into the moonlight. "You don't say." His voice was husky with need. His hot mouth encased her nipple, tongue circling the pebbled peak. "I think we need to correct that, don't you?"

"Yes," Emma answered breathlessly. Her back arched atop the covers, pressing her breasts closer to his lips. Desire coursed through her; she was just as eager and needy as she'd been this morning from the first moment Cyn had stood in her presence.

His body pressed against her, along with the unmistakable heat of his cock. She moved and bucked beneath him to better align her hips with his, but a tsking sound halted her movements.

"Not yet, sugar. You should know that by now." Cyn swooped down and ran his tongue along her slit, sucking and flicking the sensitive pearl until her thighs shook and she curled toward him.

Emma's fingers clawed the coverlet, bunching the design into a wrinkled mass. Three of Cyn's fingers played inside her, pistoning at a reckless rate. His fingers curled to prod the perfect spot. Her orgasm swelled faster than she could voice her pleasure, and seconds later, her climax soaked Cyn's skin. He placed a lingering kiss on her clit, swirling his tongue in her arousal.

"Hmm," he groaned. "I must be getting better at this to make you cum that fast."

Emma propped herself on her elbows and tilted her head. A long tendril of hair fell across her face. "Or maybe I just don't want to be teased."

Cyn's brow arched. "But the teasing is the best part."

"I disagree. Don't get me wrong, I love foreplay, but nothing beats that feeling when you slam into me so hard and deep that I forget my own name."

"Oh." Cyn's cock twitched against her. "That visual is mouthwatering." His eyes burned as he crawled up her body, a panther stalking its kill. "Should I grab you a pen and paper before I start?"

"For what?" Emma asked.

"So you can write down any important information before I fuck every thought from your beautiful mind."

Emma's lip quivered, shocked by his aggressive dirty talk. "I don't—"

"Well, in that case . . ." Without warning, Cyn flipped Emma onto her side and pushed her knees together. She gasped at the way he overpowered her body with ease. Her pussy clenched as he took charge.

"Hard and deep, right? That's what you said." Cyn's voice was caramel, smooth and rich, coming from within the shadows.

She couldn't see his face. He'd become a masked stranger with nefarious intentions. Turned on by the unexpected roughness, Emma's pulse quickened. She'd never adopted this position before. "Yes," she confirmed. She tried to push herself up, but Cyn forced her down.

Gathering her wrists in his hold, he pinned her arms above her head. Using his other hand, he spanked her exposed ass—hard. The flesh on flesh echoed with a loud smack. Her sex clenched again.

"Good. Feel free to tell me to stop . . . if you can remember *my* name."

"Have you—Oh!"

In a single thrust, Cyn buried his cock in her center, balancing on his knees to achieve the best leverage. The position caught her off guard. Her upper body twisted, and her breasts heaved with each pulse. Keeping her hands secured, Cyn spanked her again. Then he pulled her cheek to the side and drove deeper into her cunt, wrenching a moan from her lips. Emma turned her head to bury it in the mattress, but Cyn gripped her chin and forced her to look at him.

"Eyes on me, sugar. Watch as I claim your body. Watch how my length slides in and out of this wet pussy. You're mine." Another moan tore from her throat. "Say it. Say you're mine."

"I'm yours, Cyn. Claim me. Make me scream your name!"

He thrust into her again and again, drilling into her cunt from the new angle.

"Keep those eyes on me," he ordered. Her whole body bounced when he slammed into her. "Fuck, your tits look amazing like this."

"You like them?"

"The way they move every time I do this . . ." Cyn sighed through gritted teeth as he pumped even faster.

Emma felt the way her breasts rolled. Pinned as her arms were, her tits jiggled before him, enticing him closer. She whimpered when his tempo increased. The carved ridges of his abs reflected the moonlight, along with the glistening base of his cock. She only caught glimpses of it when he pulled out slightly. Her arousal shone on his shaft, claiming him as hers. There was nothing better than watching him enter her. Cyn squeezed her right breast. His fingers pinched her nipple, giving it a little jerk.

"Hey!" Emma fixed him with a surprised stare.

"Tell me to stop," Cyn challenged, pinching her again. He rolled the hard little bud between his fingers. Like the spanking, her body responded eagerly to the bite of pain.

"Harder." Emma held his gaze, staring him down as he fucked her. He continued to pull and pinch each of her nipples, meeting her demand. She groaned under the abuse, loving every second.

Grabbing her top leg, Cyn lifted it up into a full extension and pounded into her while cradling her calf against his chest. Along the curve of the muscle, he planted fiery kisses, then slowed. "Fuck, it feels so good when your cunny strokes my dick. A perfect fucking fit. You're going to make me cum, sugarcane. Where do you want it? Should I cover your tits or fill your pussy with my hot seed until it drips down your thighs?"

Emma did her best to shake her head. "No. Cum inside me. Fill me. Make me yours."

Cyn stopped thrusting and lowered her leg. Still inside her, he leaned down and stared into her eyes, sobering. "Will you truly be mine?"

"Of course—"

"No, sugar." Cyn traced the column of her throat, her jaw, her lips. "If you agree to be mine, that's it. No more threesomes or fooling around with anyone else, not even Cris. I need to keep you all to myself."

Emma replied without hesitation. "Yes."

A look of incredulity appeared on Cyn's face. "Really?"

"Yes. I've been telling you all night. As long as you don't have any cute ginger girls waiting for you back in the oven." Emma smirked, but her chest tightened. Was she really jealous of a cookie?

Cyn chuckled. "No chance of that. You're the only one I've ever wanted."

"Really? I've made some pretty stacked females."

"Trust me. None of them compared to you."

Emma smiled and brought her lips to Cyn's. They melted into a passionate kiss, getting lost in one another as lust crested, demanding to be sated. "Claim me, Cyn. In every way. I've only ever wanted to be yours."

Cyn growled against her lips, the sound animalistic. The idea of being claimed seemed so primal, but Emma loved the concept's permanence. Sure, she'd had fun with Cris, but Cyn was everything.

"Not like this, though. Let me get on top," Emma whispered.

Cyn pulled out, then, without breaking their kiss, released her cuffed hands and slid beneath her, setting her astride his lower half. His cock stood at attention, raised to full mast and shiny with her desire. "Are you ready for this?"

Emma gave a single nod. She licked her fingers, then rubbed the saliva onto her slit, readying for him once more.

"You're so sexy," Cyn said. His cock throbbed, eager to play.

Emma rose onto her knees and notched his crown exactly where she wanted him. Delicious heat ground against her clit while Cyn watched with hooded eyes. Slowly, she sank onto his shaft, inch by inch, until she'd swallowed his length. Her hips swiveled in a figure eight, luscious friction building as she rode him.

"Fuck, Emma. That feels so fucking good."

A jolt of pleasure surged through her when she heard her name in his mouth. She loved being called sugar, but her name was so intimate. Her body rocked forward and back, the grinding sensation hitting just right.

Cyn's wide hands traced the curves of her waist and settled on the swell of her ass. With both palms, he slapped and massaged the thick flesh, increasing the pressure their bodies created by elongating her strokes. His eyelids fluttered shut before he settled against the pillows, content to let her take control, but his grip never faltered.

"Holy fuck," Emma whined. Her palms planted on the mattress beside her outer thighs, and she gave herself completely to the sensual tempo, getting lost in each shuddering wave.

"This ass is mine. This pussy is mine," Cyn vowed. "This body is mine." He rolled her hips faster, causing that sensitive spot within her to vibrate. "You're mine, Emma. Mine, mine, mine, and I'm going to fuck you until the whole town hears you scream my name."

Sensing Cyn's urgency, Emma circled her hips and shifted from rocking atop his cock to bouncing. She rode to the top of his shaft only to slam back down. And she wasn't gentle. Twin groans punctuated the air, and

Cyn's grip tightened. He helped raise her up and push her back down, forcing his cock deep into her cunny.

Emma gasped each time she took his full length. This was fucking in its most basic form. Hard and fast, activating the pleasure-seeking dopamine deep inside her brain. Cyn sought to dominate, and she was more than happy to oblige his carnal drive. She slid along his cock, strained mewls and moans peppering her lips with each new thrust.

Cyn bit his lower lip. "Just like that, sugar. Take this dick like a good girl."

Emma's orgasm burned, demanding one final lick of friction. She leaned back and slammed her hips, changing his position just enough. "Oh fuck!"

"Fuck," Cyn groaned at the same time.

Together, they climbed, their climaxes in sight. Cyn's fingers burrowed into her hips, etching bruises, but Emma felt no pain. Her breasts heaved with momentum. She was a goddess, a deity, as she possessed Cyn. There were only panting breaths and pleasure between them as he prayed. Emma drove her hips down one last time. Waves of ecstasy billowed through her frame to the tips of her toes.

Simultaneously, a familiar swelling ballooned inside her, and Cyn unleashed a fierce roar. He launched off the pillows and buried his face between her breasts while he pressed her lower back closer, locking her in place. The pressure was unbelievable. Throbbing, pulsating, and vibrating all at once. Cyn ground his dick even harder into her, demanding she take him.

New ribbons of pleasure seized her. Cyn's mouth was everywhere. Licking, biting, and sucking her nipples like a starving creature of the night.

"Cyn, oh my God." The sensations were so intense. He wouldn't release her until she'd been branded as his and filled with his seed. She soon grew delirious, lost while her body was forced to experience multiple orgasms, one after another. The image of herself heavy with child sparked suddenly in her mind. No, Cyn couldn't get her pregnant, but the thought of him filling her womb with an adorable baby made her heart soar with hope nonetheless.

"Fuck, Emma. Fuck! Your cunny is so damn tight. The way you choke my dick. You're mine. You're mine, and I'm never letting you go. Say it. Be a good girl and tell me you're mine so I can fill your tight little pussy to its brim." His orders were sandpaper, rough and savage. Impossible to ignore.

The additional pressure primed her, demanding another orgasm with the finesse of a bull in a china shop. There was no rest, no end to the intense friction.

"I'm yours, Cyn. Fuck! I can't take it any longer. Fill me. Give me all of you." Emma moaned, her hair falling over her face, her body unable to escape the pressure.

Cyn roared again, and in sync, their final climaxes burst. Warmth spiked inside her while her pussy rocked, clenching his cock to milk every last drop. The feeling was indescribable, beyond any high Emma had ever experienced. A loud exhalation reverberated from Cyn's throat, confirming a similar feeling. His gaze found hers and a rush of heat coursed through her, tingling her extremities as if she'd been shocked.

"Whoa. What was that?"

Cyn shook his head, examining the back of his hand. "I'm not sure. Did I hurt you?"

"No, it was incredible. What did it feel like for you?"

Bit by bit, Cyn's cock softened and yielded its hold on her pussy. Shivers trailed her spine. Even the memory of her orgasms was enough to make her purr.

"Beyond any climax I've ever had. It was like you were made for me."

A content smile pulled at the corner of Emma's mouth. "I am a pretty good baker."

Cyn's arm snuck around her waist. Gently, he pulled her down and cradled her beside him. "And a very generous one," he added with a laugh. His lips brushed against hers and a second shock burst between them, like a small jolt of static electricity.

Emma touched her lower lip with wide eyes, but Cyn frowned. "I'm sorry. I guess we worked up quite a charge atop the sheets."

"It's okay," Emma whispered. She snuggled against his chest and was soon lulled by the steady rhythm of his heartbeat. Silence stretched, the only sound their even breaths. "I love you, Cyn. Did you know that?"

Cyn turned and pressed his lips to her forehead. "I do. Want to know how?"

"Tell me."

Cyn's long fingers scratched Emma's back in lazy circles. "Because I see the same amount of emotion in your eyes when you look at me as what exists in my own heart. You've bewitched me, body and soul."

Emma laughed and gave him a little shove. "You stole that line from the book in my bag."

"Can you blame me? It's a great line. Austen certainly knows how to charm."

"Well, keep feeding me lines and I might just sleep with you again."

"Oh please." Cyn's hand meandered down to her dripping cunt and tapped on her clit. "You love my dick just as much as I love losing myself in this cunny. We're two peas in a pod."

Emma pursed her lips and rolled to her other side, effectively disengaging Cyn's touch. "Yeah, well, I went almost two years without your big cock, so it'd be no trouble to be celibate again." She settled facing away from him, determined to prove him wrong.

Cyn's length pressed against her ass, and he breathed along the shell of her ear, his warm breath tickling the sensitive skin. "Then I'll take you from behind again. Play in that ass for as long as I like without the threat of cold water to slow me down."

At first, Emma didn't react, resolved in her use of the silent treatment. A wet smacking sound echoed in the quiet, and before she could guess at Cyn's intentions, his newly coated finger slid between her cheeks and circled the rim of her ass. "Hey!" she squealed and quickly flipped to her back. "No more for tonight! Aren't you tired? We've fucked half a dozen times." Her voice was playful, but her boundary was firm.

Walking his fingers across the plane of her stomach, Cyn grinned. "I can never get enough of you, sugar. I don't know why, but I'm suddenly flooded with energy, and there's no better way to expend it than—"

"I'm glad your dough is ready to rise again, but I'm not imbued with magical gingerbread sex powers. I'm a human who needs to get up in a few hours to take on a mustached menace, so there shall only be cuddling and unconsciousness in this bed for the rest of the evening."

"Yup. I love it when you're bossy."

"Good. Then change the sheets while I run to the bathroom. I can't begin to imagine the mess we've made. Clean sheets are in the bottom drawer of the dresser." Emma peeled back the covers and slipped out of bed, her nakedness illuminated by the silver moonlight.

"Wow," Cyn breathed. "You look like you've been dusted in sugar."

Emma glanced down and only saw white-blue moonlight reflecting off her pale flesh, but the way Cyn's eyes lit with wonder made her feel beautiful and confident. "Thank you." She leaned onto the mattress and kissed him, slow and sensual. "I'll be right back. Then you can keep this little sugar crystal's bad dreams at bay."

# CHAPTER TWELVE

The morning dawned golden and clear. Sunlight streamed through the frosted glass, caressing Emma's eyelids. She arched her back and stretched like a contented cat. Upon her movement, strong arms cinched around her middle and held her in place. With a languid chirp, she scrunched back toward Cyn's chest and inhaled. The scent of cedar and musk infiltrated her senses. Something tickled at the back of her mind but was quickly forgotten when Cyn covered her neck and collarbone with a parade of kisses.

"Morning." Cyn nuzzled her tangled golden mane.

"Morning. I could get used to this." Emma rolled to face him and kissed the tip of his nose. "Waking up next to you. Did you sleep well?"

"Mm-hmm. Like a baby. You?"

"I did. Though, I'm surprised. If I'm too hot, I toss and turn all night. I was worried your heat would be too much, but I hardly noticed." Emma trailed her fingers down Cyn's tricep. His skin didn't emanate the same powerful blast she was accustomed to, but maybe sleeping beside him all night had acclimated her.

"You were exhausted," Cyn pointed out. "All that wild sex."

"Which was your fault, by the way."

"I didn't hear any complaints. The only instructions I heard were '*harder*' and '*faster*.'"

"Stop it!" Emma wriggled against him and playfully pushed off his chest.

"Maybe you can work on rejecting more of my advances today." Cyn cupped her breast and gave it a firm squeeze before his thumb circled the rosy bud in its center.

Emma leaned into his touch and fluttered her lashes while desire spread to the apex of her thighs. "Or I could use you until I'm satisfied first." Her hand wove between them and wrapped around Cyn's soft cock.

"Oh no. Don't do that. Someone help me," Cyn called sarcastically.

Emma threw her head back and laughed. She urged her hand up and down his length, marveling when it thickened and throbbed beneath her touch. Maybe she had magic powers after all.

Cyn shifted onto his back and flung his arm over his face. "Fuck, sugarcane. The things you do to me." A minute later, his cock stood fully engorged and erect, straining under the sheets.

After yanking the covers away, Emma slid down and crawled between Cyn's legs. His shaft throbbed at her proximity and grazed her lip. "Oh, is he trying to tell me something?"

"To open those pretty lips and suck it—in the nicest way possible," Cyn explained with a crooked smirk.

Emma tilted her head. "Suck it? Like, put it in my mouth?"

"Yes," Cyn ordered.

"How much?" Emma tossed her mussed hair, and the sunlight shone on her peaked nipples.

"All of it."

Emma's brow rose. "All of it? But it's too big."

"I don't care. Stick out your tongue."

Dutifully, Emma's pink tongue popped between her lips.

"Good girl. Now, lick the head."

Emma leaned forward and ran her tongue along the smooth tip, tracing the veins that ran along the shaft until Cyn groaned. "Did I do it right?" she asked with innocent eyes.

"You're driving me fucking crazy, sugar. This time, open your mouth wider and take it on your tongue so it glides to the back of your throat."

Emma shimmied her chest and held her breasts in her hands, pushing them together while she pretended to consider his words. "Okay, so lick it and put it all in my mouth."

"Now." Cyn's command was hardly audible as he spoke through gritted teeth. "I need you to suck this dick."

She released her breasts and resumed her position between his legs. His cock was rock hard, desperate for her lips. Emma kissed the shining slit, and a salty flavor grazed her tongue. "You taste different." She leaned closer and inhaled. His cinnamon scent was nowhere to be found. When she awoke, she'd dismissed it as nothing, but now, it was definitely missing. Her hands slid down his thighs. The temperature of his skin matched hers rather than radiating its usual heat. Strange, but it *was* early. She needed coffee. Clearly, she was imagining things.

"Please, sugar," Cyn begged.

Distracted from her thoughts by his obvious distress, Emma softened her jaw and slid her mouth over the crown of his cock. She hummed when she pulled her cheeks in and started to suck.

"Fuck, yes." Cyn's fingers tangled in her hair. Her intent was to go slowly, draw out his climax for as long as possible, but already she'd driven him past the point of patience. While pumping his hips, Cyn pushed the back of her head farther down his length, forcing his cock behind her teeth until he hit the back of her throat. "Fuck, sugar. Right there. Choke on this big dick." He pushed even harder, making her gag before he released her.

Emma spat the excess saliva onto the tip and took a quick breath before Cyn thrust back inside her mouth. Using two hands, he brushed the hair out of her face and moved his hips, fucking her mouth while her big amber eyes stared up at him.

"Shit, Emma. You're so fucking good at that."

Emma moaned low in her throat. She loved watching him come undone beneath her touch. Without meaning to, her gaze wandered to the left, to the small clock on the wall. Panic flared. She reared back and broke free of Cyn's hold.

Cyn reached for her body. "You ready to ride this dick now?"

Emma shook her head and pointed at the time. "It's almost ten! I had no idea. I'm so late! Nicoli said he'd be at the shop first thing in the morning. This is only going to strengthen his case against me. Cyn, we have to go!" Cyn leapt into action while Emma tore open her dresser and threw on the first dress her searching hands encountered. "In the closet, I bought a few pants and shirts for you in case you ever came back. I had to guess at the sizes, so I hope something fits."

"You bought all this for me on the off chance that I'd come back?" Cyn wondered.

Color flushed Emma's cheeks. If she weren't running so late, she'd be crumpling with embarrassment at his question. Did buying clothes for a fictional man make her unhinged? To pine so badly for someone logic dictated she'd never see again? Would this small act finally convince Cyn she was delusional?

"I wanted you to be comfortable." Emma averted her gaze and hurriedly donned a new pair of panties before stretching on sheer tights. "I know that's weird, and you probably think I'm strange, but—"

"Emma." Cyn's calm steadying timbre halted her frenzied movements. He crossed the room and cradled her face in his hands. "Your heart knows no bounds. Thank you." He swept her up in a sweet kiss, nuzzling her nose with his own. "Everything will be fine, sugar."

Threading her fingers through his, Emma nodded. His promise soothed the anxious fluttering in her chest a fraction, but she was still a bundle of nerves. Her prayers had been answered at last and delivered Cyn to her once again, but their future was fragile, hanging in the balance against one man's greed.

"I hope so." Her eyes flickered back to the clock hands that ticked even faster toward the unknown.

The bakery's brick façade contrasted with the crisp white snow. A ribbon of steam curled from the skinny chimney. Had Cris opened for customers? Emma raced, as ladylike as possible, through the barely cleared streets, thankful for her high boots as she tramped through the icy layers that had frozen overnight. Cyn paced behind, letting her take the lead. She loved the night they'd spent together, but it had left her with no time to prepare a defense against Henry's nephew. Like everything else lately, she was going to have to wing it.

A flurry of wind kicked up a few stray leaves that had managed to evade winter's blanket. Emma raised her hands to shield her face from their withered touch but stopped short when her friend Jane exited her shop. Her presence there wasn't abnormal—she usually popped by to visit at least once throughout the day—but an odd look dazzled in her eyes, and her reddened cheeks spoke of having little to do with the brisk temperature.

"Morning, Jane. Sorry, I overslept. Was there anything you needed?" Emma considered her friend's empty hands. "If you don't mind cookies from yesterday, I can give you a few of those."

Jane's moss-green eyes found hers as her fingers fumbled with the thin gold chain around her neck. Was it the shadows the sun cast or did her friend's skin appear slightly bruised? Emma dismissed her musings. After all, she'd thought there was something different about Cyn, too. It had to be the agitated state she'd riled herself into.

"Oh no. I just dropped in to say hello and check how the rest of your evening went," Jane answered with a knowing smirk. "Judging by your company, I'd say it was . . . energetic to say the least."

Emma bit her lower lip and eyed Cyn in her periphery. "Are you free for lunch sometime next week? Unfortunately, I'll have quite a bit of leisure time if my next meeting goes south."

A sour frown darkened Jane's gaze. "Does that have anything to do with the vile little man waiting for you? He interrupted us, and—" Jane stifled her speech with a gloved hand. "What I meant to say was, he thought I was you with Cris in the kitchen and rudely waltzed back there like he owned the place."

Shivers tickled the nape of Emma's neck. "He's trying to obtain ownership of the bakery. He's Henry's nephew. Even from beyond the grave, that man has found a way to wound me. Hang on . . . Why were you in the kitchen?"

Scarlet flamed across Jane's face, causing her rosy cheeks to stand out even more boldly against her beige complexion. "Oh, nothing really. Cris was taking a fresh batch of oatmeal raisins out of the oven and invited me to partake in a . . . free sample."

"I bet he did," said Cyn, speaking for the first time. "That's when Nicoli interrupted the two of you? When you were eating cookies?"

Jane clasped her unbuttoned collar and pressed it to her throat. "Yes, I just said that. Well, he's been in there giving Cris an earful for twenty minutes now. I tried to help him stall until you arrived and volunteered to stop by your house. Thank goodness I ran into you first. I'd like to come back later and check on Cris if that's all right?"

Emma grinned a tight-lipped smirk. She recognized the yearning look in her friend's stare and the way her chest heaved with desire. "Of course, Jane. Whenever you wish. I'll make sure Cris takes a long break so you two can . . . talk." She widened her eyes, silently communicating she knew exactly what kind of cookies Cris had baked and that she wasn't going to let Jane off the hook until she spilled every detail.

Jane gave a subtle nod and made her exit. "Much appreciated. Till then. Good luck with skippy in there."

Cyn offered a gentlemanly bow, and Emma brushed her friend's arm when she passed. She prayed the two new lovers hadn't made too big of a mess.

Once Jane was on her way, Cyn gestured toward the door. "Are you ready?"

Emma took a steadying breath. "I suppose."

"Remember, I'm right here."

She exhaled, and a cloud of vapor coalesced in the air. "Let's go." Emma strode into the bakery, holding her head high. She refused to be chased out of her own shop with her tail between her legs by this tiny insignificant fraction of a man.

"You're back!" Cris cleared his throat. "I mean, morning, Boss. I gotta tell ya, I thought I could do this early shift, but it's for the birds. You were right."

"It's okay, Cris. Thanks for covering for me, but I've got this." Emma patted his forearm and pivoted on her thick heels. The love seat where she, Cris, and Cyn had enjoyed their first threesome was the target of her attention. At the present moment, the cushions held a far less enticing sight.

Nicoli sat with one leg crossed over the other at the knee, bowler hat balanced on the tip of his Oxford shoe. He set down the newspaper he'd been pretending to read with a flourish and tossed it into a crumpled heap. After fixing his hat atop his head, he stood to his full height to bring himself level with her. Nicoli glanced at his golden watch and made a tsking sound in the back of his throat.

"Nearly 10:00 a.m. Is this the schedule you keep? Do you honestly expect me to believe this mess-ridden shop actually makes a profit?" Nicoli heaved a long sigh. "Not to worry, my dear. I have a signed order from the local courthouse stating this bakery and all future profits revert to me." He waved the document before

Emma's eyes, careful to keep it out of her reach. "I'm here to rid you of this headache and provide for you as my beloved uncle did." His eyes gleamed, lips curling in a deceitful smirk.

"Did you ever meet Henry?" Emma asked. "If I were to hazard a guess, I'd say your father no doubt heard about his brother's passing and told you how to stake your claim, hoping to siphon what he could of Henry's estate. I don't believe you even went abroad. I'd bet you were destitute, living on scraps. And rather than introduce yourself and kindly ask for a job, you chose instead to strong-arm me and manipulate the law to give you the whole pie instead. Am I warm?"

"Ding, ding. We have a winner. I must admit I underestimated you. Seems there's a bit of an intelligent scrapper behind all those dick cookies. Guess there's more than meets the slutty eye."

"That's enough," Cyn seethed, stepping in front of her.

Nicoli appraised Cyn's towering figure. "You're very intimidating. You and your shorter twin over there." He took a step closer until he was toe to toe with the gingerbread man. "But move out of my way, pal. I've got business to conclude."

For a moment, Cyn didn't respond. Instead, he exhaled through his nostrils like a bull and steeled his jaw. "How would you like to drink through a straw for the next six weeks, *pal*?"

A bewildered gasp choked in Nicoli's throat. "Are you threatening me, sir? Why don't I get the police and ask for their interpretation?"

"No, no, stop!" Emma stepped between them. "Your business is with me, Dunst." She turned to Cyn and softened her tone. "I can fight my own battles, even against a troll."

Nicoli pressed his hand to his heart. "Ouch. How will I ever recover from that? Here are the papers. Either get out or get to work. This bakery is mine. You can also hand over your house key. I expect a warm meal at suppertime and then who knows what the night will bring us?"

"I'm not giving you anything," Emma hissed.

"Is that so? Perhaps I'll refer you to the asylum instead. It's the perfect place for ornery women who talk back and disrespect their husbands. Seems you need their . . . guidance."

Emma raised her chin. "I won't let you do this to me."

Nicoli's laughter ricocheted off the walls, loud and unsettling as gunshots. "Oh no? You won't let me? Look around, sweetheart. It's already done, and there's nothing you can do to change that."

"Want to bet?" Cris's strong voice boomed from the display case. In his hand, a piece of slightly wrinkled paper fluttered. "Emma isn't powerless against you despite your attempts to gaslight her."

Nicoli sneered. "What are you talking about?"

"The judge only granted you the executor of the estate because he was operating under the assumption that Emma is a single woman, and because of your antiquated laws, unmarried women do not possess the right to own property."

"As fascinating as this history lesson is—"

"However, Emma is *not* single. I hold in my hand a marriage certificate with her name listed. All it requires is to be notarized and her marriage is legal and binding—consequently negating that piece of shit you're clinging so tightly to," Cris finished with a wide grin.

"Marriage? To whom?" Nicoli shouted. "She's a widow. Has been for years."

"Me," Cyn stated. "Emma is *my* wife. Mine."

Emma's heart soared at the power of his declaration. He hadn't just been telling her what she wanted to hear last night. He'd meant every word. He was ready to solidify their union forever.

"This is absurd!" Nicoli blustered. "You can't marry her!"

"I already did. As my brother said, all that's left is to have it notarized and filed."

Nicoli scoffed and fixed his hands on his hips. He dropped his head and shook it back and forth. "Well, I suppose that's that. I'm out of plays, it would seem. Unless—" He raced over to where Cris stood, hands transforming into claws as he swiped and slashed at the document.

"Hey!" Cris yelled. Dodging the crazed attack, he leapt onto the counter beside the register and jumped off, landing in a shoulder roll on the floor.

Cyn raced after Nicoli and wrestled him to the ground, pinning his thrashing arms behind his back. "I'll hold him off! Take Emma and get that thing signed. Hurry!"

"Got it!" Cris offered a crisp salute, then ushered Emma out the door and onto the sidewalk. "Where to?"

Her friend's sweet smile leapt to her mind. "Jane! She's a notary. We have to get to the library."

# CHAPTER THIRTEEN

Cris grabbed Emma's hand and pulled her down the street, dodging dogs, benches, and startled people as they ran.

"How do you know the way?" Emma asked breathlessly after they rounded the second corner.

"She said it was two rights and up a hill," Cris answered.

"Who said?"

"Jane. We talked for a bit earlier."

"About her working part-time at the library?" Emma said doubtfully.

"Last night, I may have snuck into the city clerk's office and found a marriage license for you."

Emma gasped. "You stole it?"

"No, it's just a blank form. During office hours, they give these things away. I may have broken in, but I only took the form. When neither you nor Cyn showed up on time, I worried that guy beat you to the punch, so I filled it out just in case."

"Thank you." Emma was touched by his

thoughtfulness. "How did you know about all that stuff back there? You sounded so official."

"Hey . . . You might think I'm just a gorgeous physique, but I pay attention."

"You were amazing." They slowed their pace once they reached the bottom of the hill. "So, you just happened to mention your plight to Jane when she stopped in for cookies this morning?"

Cris shrugged, his cheeks tinging with color. "I wasn't trying to be sneaky. I asked if she knew how the town legalized marriages, and that's when she told me about notaries. I should have asked her to sign it right there, but she didn't have her stamp thing, and then Nicoli barged in."

Their conversation ceased as they hoofed it up to the top of the next hill. The small clapboard building that served as their library stood in the center beside a tiny pond. In the summertime, Emma brought stale and leftover pastries to share with the sweet mallards and their ducklings.

"Was that why Jane looked so flushed when I arrived? All that talk of notary business and city clerk processes?" Emma asked once they reached the front doors.

Cris shot another bashful glance over his shoulder. "She wasn't exactly forthcoming with all the information."

"You don't say. A stranger demanding her help ensuring her best friend's marriage to a guy she's never even met? And what did you do when she refused to talk? Fuck it out of her?" Emma suggested.

"Something like that." Cris winked. "We made a deal. She would give me one answer in exchange for one act of her choosing. The game escalated kind of quickly."

Emma imagined her poor unsuspecting friend dueling with Cris in a sexually charged stand-off. Jane, like herself, had been single for years and was considered an old maid in society's eyes. Emma supposed Jane had asked for a kiss, and boy did Cris deliver. Her mind jumped to Cyn's readiness this morning. Were these gingerbread men ever satisfied?

Emma cleared her throat. "This will be interesting, then."

Cris held open the door for Emma to pass through first, and their pounding strides quieted to soft footfalls. Only two or three people combed the stacks for their next read. Jane sat behind the oak desk in the center of the room, adjusting the reading glasses perched on the end of her nose. At Emma's approach, her friend's blank expression broke into a genuine smile, but her eyes flared wide when she caught sight of Cris's large silhouette behind her.

"What are you doing here?" Jane asked in a hushed voice, suddenly ignoring Emma altogether.

Cris sidled up to the desk and leaned his elbows on the smooth surface. "I wanted to see you again."

Emma noted the way his timbre dropped, the notes rich with desire. The earlier burn immediately rewarmed Jane's cheeks.

"You just saw *plenty* of me," Jane hissed in response.

"You had fun though, right? At least, it seemed like you did."

Jane yanked the sleeves of her dress over her hands, effectively hiding them from view. She licked her lips and cast a furtive glance around them in case of nearby listeners. "Of course, but I'm not sure what we did is even legal in the state of Pennsylvania."

"It is where I'm from."

"And where's that? You still haven't told me."

"Your dreams, Janey."

Jane leaned over the desk, fingers gripping the edge. "I am at work right now. You can't—"

"Hey, Jane." Emma waved to direct Jane's attention. "He's actually here because we need a favor. Can you please notarize this? We're in a hurry." She offered a quick smile, but her heart was racing. How long could Cyn contain Nicoli? What if a customer walked in and saw them fighting? What if, when she returned, all she found were crumbs? She shoved the document forward and bounced on her toes.

"Yeah, sure." Jane righted the form and briefly perused it. A moment later, her eyebrows nearly disappeared in her hairline. "You need this notarized for the both of you?" Her voice was tinny, high-pitched, hardly more than a squeak. The rosy blooms of color on her cheeks darkened to a fiery crimson.

"Please. That'd be great," Emma said.

Cris nodded, but his easy charm faded when he registered the rage in Jane's eyes. "Oh crumbs, no! It's not what you think." He waved his hands in front of his face, shouting far louder than anyone should in a library. The other occupants looked up from their novels in favor of the drama unfolding before their eyes.

"You mean to tell me you fucked me like a dog—splayed out on my hands and knees—while you're engaged to my best friend? Why didn't you tell me *you* were her mystery man?"

"Oh my God!" Emma cried, suddenly understanding her friend's hostile attitude.

"No! No! You've got it all wrong, Jane," Cris said.

"Oh, do I? So this isn't your name beside Emma's? What was all that this morning? Emma, I'm so sorry. If I had known—"

"Shit! I didn't realize. It was late. I meant to write my brother's." Cris grabbed the form and erased his name as Emma pushed him to the side.

"Jane, it's okay. I'm not marrying Cris. We did fuck a few times yesterday, but it didn't mean any—"

"What?" Jane's eyes were as wide as dinner plates.

"I promise I will explain everything over several bottles of wine. Cyn, my actual fiancé who you saw me with this morning, is waiting for me and is caught in a pretty precarious situation." Glancing at Cris's correction, Emma grabbed the document and thrust it in front of her friend once more. "So, if you will please just notarize this, I can be on my way and go get him," she nearly pleaded.

Everyone, including the library patrons listening, held a collective breath. At last, Jane cracked a smile and retrieved her stamp from a drawer. She fit the form into the raised stamp machine and pounded down on the top. Tight-lipped, she slid the document out to assess the seal.

"Here you go." Jane handed it to Emma and finally raised her eyes to her friend. The anger was gone, replaced with burning curiosity.

Emma sighed. "Thank you so much." She cradled the paper safely to her chest. "I'm sorry I can't explain right now, but I will. Promise." After pivoting in a militant fashion, she retreated to the door, practically running.

Behind her, Cris said something, but it was too low to decipher. Hopefully, Jane would give him another chance. They made a very cute couple, and it'd be great if Cris found someone now that she and Cyn were official. She still couldn't believe it. She'd wanted to be with him for so long, and finally, finally, she would have the fairy tale ending she was denied two years ago. That is, if she got the marriage license to the clerk in time.

"Cris, we have to go!" He hesitated for a few seconds longer at Jane's desk but managed to catch up before the door swung closed. "Patch things up?"

"Enough for her to agree to see me again," he replied with a beaming smile.

Emma trotted down the slope, the form clutched in her hand. The last thing she needed was an errant breeze to blow it out of her reach. "I'm happy to hear that. Now, can you lead the way to the clerk's office? The last time I was there was two years ago, and I was pretty distraught.

"You got it."

They ran in silence, retracing their steps around the first corner. However, instead of following the road back the way they'd come, Cris led her to the left to a square building beside a milliner's shop. A rusted sign read *City Clerk* in tarnished lettering. "Took me a hell of a long time to find this place. So, you were really shaken up after losing my brother, huh?"

Emma slowed her pace to a walk and caught her breath. "Yes. It was horrific to see him die like that. Here was this incredible man I thought I'd literally dreamed up. Then, after spending an amazing day together, he not only gets eaten by my husband but proceeds to crumble to cookie dust in my lap. If it hadn't been for Jane's support, I don't think I would have made it this long."

She reached for the dingy handle but a warm hand on her shoulder made her pause. Cris regarded her with a stoic expression, black eyebrows furrowed. She'd never seen such a serious countenance on his face before.

"What is it?" Emma asked, fearful they'd forgotten something.

"I'm sorry you had to endure that alone. I know my brother and can see how ardently he cares for you. If he'd had a choice, he never would have left. You know that, right?"

Emma nodded and blinked back tears. "Yes, but that's very sweet of you to say." She rubbed his hand, and they shared a smile. "I'm glad you decided to stick around. It's been . . . fun getting to know you."

Cris's intensity softened and the familiar grin took its place. "Same here . . . sis."

"Ew. Never call me that again."

An uncomfortable chuckle reverberated in his chest. "You're right. Way too weird. Now, let's get inside and—" His words evaporated when he caught sight of something over her shoulder. "Oh crumbs."

"What?" Emma followed the direction of his gaze.

Nicoli was sprinting toward them. A rivulet of blood decorated his chin from a split lip. Not far behind, Cyn's feet stomped the snow, arms pumping as he fought to catch up. Disjointed syllables carried on the wind, but he was too far away for Emma to make them out.

"What did he say?"

"I can't be positive, but I think he's telling us to get our asses inside." Cris pushed her across the threshold and into the stuffy lobby. A balding man with large spectacles jumped at their sudden intrusion.

"Are you the city clerk? Emma asked.

The man fixed his glasses and blinked, appearing owllike behind the lenses. "Yes, what can I—"

"I need to file this marriage license immediately." Emma thrust the document at him. "We've had it notarized and everything."

The man picked up the form and studied the text. "Indeed you have. Is this the groom?"

"Uh, no, but he's on his way. He'll be here any min—"

"Stop right there!" Nicoli's sharp voice cut through the small office. "This woman is trying to commit fraud!"

"No, I'm not."

The door slammed open again a moment later, permitting Cyn's muscular frame into the already shrinking space. A scarlet gash carved his eyebrow and blood dripped into his eye.

"I'm sorry, Emma. He got hold of a steel spatula and swung at me. By the time I got to my feet, he was out the door," Cyn explained under his breath.

Emma examined his wound from across the crowded space. It looked superficial, thank goodness, but painful. "There's nothing to be sorry for. This kind gentleman was just asking for you, and I was in the midst of telling him you'd be right along." She faced the clerk and turned on her megawatt smile. "See? He's nothing if not prompt."

"And a fake," Nicoli snarled. "That man is a fraud she's trying to pass off as her husband to undermine my claim to her bakery. This so-called marriage is a sham. That property, along with my late uncle's house, rightfully belongs to me." He held up a severely crumpled piece of paper and slammed it onto the clerk's desk. "Read for yourself."

With careful movements, the clerk pored over the newest form. The tension in the room was palpable, thick enough to cut and serve. Cyn brushed Nicoli out of the way to stand beside Emma. His hands threaded with hers and he kissed her on the forehead.

"You're hurt," Emma whispered. She dragged the pad of her thumb gingerly along the puckered ridge of the wound, nervous it might be deeper than she'd originally thought.

"I'm fine," Cyn said. "He barely scraped me."

Her hand drifted down to Cyn's jaw and cupped his face. "You promised you wouldn't leave me again."

Cyn kissed her palm. "And I intend to keep that promise."

"Good."

The clerk released a dry cough, with both documents at eye level. His eyes ping-ponged back and forth, reading each line by line. He inhaled a shaky breath and scrunched his nose. "It seems to me that Ms. Emma, seeing as how she was the first to enter my office, is entitled to keep both the business and the home she shared with her late husband. Though your last name is missing on the license, dear." He passed the document back to her and pointed to the blank space.

"No! This is preposterous! Look at them. Don't you see? This is an act! A charade! Don't let them play you, good sir." Nicoli radiated rage.

The clerk raised his bushy salt-and-pepper eyebrows and crossed his arms over his chest. "They seem like a lovely couple whose only crime is to be unfortunately associated with you."

Nicoli opened his mouth to argue, but the clerk threw up his hand and continued before he could utter a single syllable.

"Now, I have heard of Ms. Emma's bakery. My wife adores her cheeky pastries. As far as I'm concerned, she's a pillar of the community, doing what she can to improve this town."

"By making pornographic lude cookies? She belongs in jail for creating such disgusting things, not celebrated," Nicoli spat venomously.

"And what have you done young man? What are your contributions to our society? Ms. Emma's cookies bring joy to everyone who sees them and remind old geezers like me how beautiful my wife is and how lucky I am to have a loving woman willing to put up with me for so long. Frankly, I'm more concerned with your level of outrage regarding a baked good, as well as your entitled assumption that you're seemingly better than this woman who has worked so hard to run that bakery. Just because you have nothing going on in your life and are more miserable than a child with a lint-covered lollipop doesn't mean you have the right to tear her down and make her as miserable as you are."

"But—But—" Nicoli stammered.

"Ms. Emma, if you could please fill in your legal name here," the clerk asked gently. He raised his brow and fixed Nicoli with a stern look over the rim of his glasses. "As for you, kindly vacate my office before I call the sheriff."

Nicoli's eyes flared. For a second, his chest swelled with indignation, but then Cyn and Cris both turned and glared, like two bodybuilders capturing him in their crosshairs. Without another retort, he slammed the bowler onto his head and stormed out the door, shutting it with a wild slam.

"Youths," the clerk said with a shake of his head. "I do hope he finds some manners out there, or better yet, someone levels him with a good hard dose of reality in the form of a swift kick to the rear."

"I believe you already did that, sir." Emma giggled and accepted the pen from his wrinkled fingers.

"Let's hope the lesson sticks with him, then. Right there, dear." The clerk pointed.

"Silly me. In all the excitement, I must have forgotten to print it. There," Emma said with a grateful smile. She handed the pen back and took a step backward into Cyn's waiting arms.

The clerk spun the document right side up and double-checked each line. "Excellent. Everything is now complete. As of this moment, you two are now recognized as Mr. and Mrs. Spice. This license is valid for ninety days. Once my office receives a signature from a minister or justice of the peace, your marriage certificate will be mailed promptly. You also retain the rights to both your bakery and your home."

"Yes!" Cris pumped his fist into the air.

Cyn whirled Emma in a tight circle and captured her lips in a passionate kiss. Squealing with delight, she wrapped her arms around his neck and pressed her body as close as possible against him.

"Good to see such joy and two people clearly head over heels for one another. But if your party doesn't mind, Mrs. Spice, I am just about to close for lunch. My wife made me a pastrami sandwich that is calling my name."

"Of course, sir. Thank you so much. Please relay to your wife that she is entitled to free pastries for life," Emma said.

The clerk inclined his head and grinned. "That is very kind of you, Mrs. Spice. I wish you and your husband a happy forever." He gestured toward the door and pushed his glasses back onto the bridge of his nose. "Have a lovely day."

# CHAPTER FOURTEEN

The moment the trio congregated outside, Cris swooped down and pulled Emma into a big hug, lifting her feet off the ground. There was no sign of Nicoli. No doubt the coward ran off toward the station, hoping to catch the first train out after his gamble backfired.

Cris returned Emma to the sidewalk and sighed. "I can't believe we pulled that off! What now?" He turned toward the couple, who'd once again found themselves in each other's arms, two magnets determined to collide, no matter the obstacle.

Emma shrugged. "I guess we plan a wedding and have a party to celebrate. If that's what you want?" She gazed up at Cyn. She knew he loved her, but was he willing to publicize their relationship even with his worries about permanence?

"The sooner, the better," Cyn answered before kissing her. "That is, if you don't mind being married to a cookie."

Emma laughed, but the joke quickly fell flat. Her mirth dried up, and she stared at Cyn as if truly seeing him for the first time. Suddenly, the itching that had been wriggling around at the back of her brain all morning burst. "But you're not a cookie. Not anymore."

"What are you talking about?" Cyn asked, wrinkling his brow.

Emma ran her hands along his frame and blinked in bewilderment. "I thought I noticed something different about you earlier. In bed, you smelled odd—not in a bad way, but your cinnamon scent was missing. And when we were fooling around, you tasted different too. Your usual sweet vanilla flavor was gone. And now, after Nicoli hit you, you're bleeding."

"Because Nicoli cut him with a spatula," Cris said.

Emma waved her hands. "But that's just it! When Henry bit you, your skin changed back into gingerbread, remember? Even after he mangled your neck and ear, there was never any blood, only crumbs and dust. But now you're . . . human."

Cyn regarded her with a baffled expression as he fought for something to say. "I don't understand. How? What did we do differently this time?"

Emma bit her lip. Memories of the night before fluttered in her mind's eye: the image of them cuddling in the moonlight, their joint admissions that lust had evolved into love. Was it as simple as that?

"I told you I loved you last night," Emma whispered. "I chose to be yours. Only yours."

Cyn's brow furrowed around the hardening gash. "So when you agreed to be mine . . . I became human?"

A slow smile grew on Emma's face. "Maybe? I think

so. Like true love's first kiss in the fairy tales. Maybe we never needed to figure the magic out. We just needed love to keep you here with me."

"More like true love's vow of monogamy, but hey, if it works . . ." Cris shrugged.

Emma shoved him with narrowed eyes, then turned back to Cyn, a full-blooded human man, no cinnamon or icing in sight. "So, this is real, right? I'm not dreaming?" Emma asked.

"As a literal cookie brought to life, I think I can believe in the power of true love." Cyn chuckled. "No, sugar, you're not dreaming. You're wide awake and all mine . . . forever."

He lifted her off the ground, and Emma hooked her legs around his waist, cradling his face in her hands. "So, you're staying? You're staying with me?"

"For as long as you'll have me, Mrs. Spice."

Emma squealed and kissed him, not stopping to even draw a breath. Joy radiated through her chest as if her heart had been replaced by a miniature sun. Eventually, they broke apart, and she pressed her forehead to his. After the transformation, Cyn had retained his tattoos, but they no longer shimmered with the promise of flavored icing.

"I'm so happy, Cyn. Though I will say, I'm going to miss you smelling of cinnamon and tasting like vanilla and marshmallow." Her gaze flickered lower, and she tilted her head with a smirk.

Cyn's lips captured hers, his tongue delving into her mouth to dance with her own. The sensuality of it caused her sex to clench. She wanted him so badly, to physically solidify and celebrate their love. Would he be opposed to taking her in the street? She eyed the alley separating the milliner's and clerk's offices. Adrenaline surged, and her heart rate spiked as she pictured Cyn balancing her against the brick wall and pounding into her. Without Emma realizing it, her hips started to roll against his torso, begging to play.

"Just because I no longer smell or taste delicious doesn't mean we can't incorporate frosting or spices into our sex life." Cyn spanked her ass, then caressed the tender spot. "You do own a bakery, after all."

Emma felt him thicken beneath her. Saw the way his pupils blew wide with lust. Eagerly, she nodded and pointed to the alley before her hand slid into the waistband of his pants. The crown of his cock met her palm, straining for her touch.

"Over there," Emma instructed around Cyn's lips.

Cyn groaned in her mouth and palmed her ass beneath her dress. Tracing her curves, he breathed huskily in her ear. "I don't know if I can make that. I need you right now, Mrs. Spice."

His admission was a powder keg, driving Emma wild with desire. She pushed the top of his pants lower to expose more of his thick length, hiding her movements with her long dress. She gave his shaft a squeeze and Cyn cursed.

"Fuck, my wife is so naughty."

"And horny beyond belief. We never did finish what we started this morning." She sank lower in his arms to better align herself. "I need you inside me." She shimmied her tights down her thighs just enough, then yanked her panties to the side. Cyn's cock nudged her clit.

"Crumbs. I didn't realize you were so wet." Holding his cock in one hand, Cyn bounced Emma on his hip and thrust into her warm center.

"Yes!" she cried. Cyn walked toward the alley, raining kisses over her lips and neck. "Hurry," Emma moaned in his ear. She rocked her hips to take him deeper and create the friction she so desperately needed.

"Fuck, sugar. I can't move when you do that." Cyn groaned but continued shuffling his feet. The alley was so close.

"Yeah, well, you two have fun and enjoy. I can see that you already are, so I'm going to get out of here and see if I can rattle some library shelves with my naughty notary." His words paused as they traveled farther away. "And you haven't heard a word I've said." Cris finished with a laugh. He didn't wait for an acknowledgment before he rounded the corner, out of sight.

The cold brick wall slammed into Emma's back, but she felt nothing except the added pressure as the jolt drove Cyn deeper. She braced her arms over his shoulders to cement her grip. Cyn nibbled her earlobe, then found her lips again. They were both so hungry for the other. She bucked her hips, but Cyn stood as motionless as a sentry, withdrawing his cock to the tip. She narrowed her eyes and wiggled her hips in demand.

"I love you, Emma," Cyn said with a knowing grin, fully aware he was driving her mad. "Will you marry me?" At last, he thrust into her, rough and raw.

Emma moaned in pleasure. Cyn thrust again, increasing his rhythm. Her back hit the wall, and her exposed ass where her dress rode up rubbed the brick as he took her, satisfying her ache.

"That's not an answer," Cyn growled. He withdrew again and pressed his crown to her clit, drilling it so fast she could hardly catch her breath from the way her orgasm roiled to the surface. He swore and thrust back into her pussy, gripping her hips as hard as he could. She'd have bruises tonight, but she didn't care.

"Yes, Cyn! Yes! I'll marry you!"

"That's my good girl." Faster and rougher, he fucked her, groaning as Emma rode his cock. Her nails dug into his skin. After so many nights lying alone with a broken heart, fingers sore from sculpting dough and burned from the oven, her gingerbread man was back, and nothing would ever separate them again.

# ACKNOWLEDGMENTS

I would like to start by thanking every single person who took the time to read the first installment of Emma and Cyn's story. Without your feedback, excitement, and demand for more, this sequel would never have been written. I hope you enjoyed this pun-filled ride with the same satisfaction as a cold glass of milk. To my brilliant editor Chelsea Cambeis, thank you for diving back into this naughty fairy tale with me. Your little emoji comments had me crying. To my friend and cover designer Neil J Hart, I am constantly blown away by your talent to transform a rough idea in my head into stunning artwork. Hopefully this will be the year for the Bills or the 49ers! To one of my closest author friends and proofreader, Samanatha Moran, thank you for answering every random thought I text you and polishing my words until they shine. I would be lost without you. To my children, Jack and Joanna, I adore all the time we get to spend together. Your input and opinions on all my projects are so special to me. I can't wait to read your own books someday. Lastly, to my husband, Daniel. We've created the perfect life together and I can't wait for all our adventures still to come.

## ABOUT THE AUTHOR

Caytlyn Brooke is a multi-award-winning author and is slowly getting better about writing happy endings. A graduate of UAlbany with a degree in psychology, it was a Grimm fairy tale course that reignited her love of creating her own twisted tales. She lives in Elmira, NY with her husband, two children, and an eternally chonky cat. Though a terrible baker, her favorite dessert is a warm chocolate brownie topped with vanilla ice cream and caramel sauce.